Ghosts
and
More
Ghosts

"Some of my best friends are ghosts, and I am adding these to the list. A choice blend of ghostly gooseflesh and ectoplasmic entertainment."

—ALFRED HITCHCOCK

These ten stories, written by an expert in the art of the strange, the spooky, and the suspenseful, will give you hours of pleasantly shivery reading—mixed with chuckles to relieve the tension.

Ghosts
and
More
Ghosts

Robert Arthur

Illustrated by Irv Docktor

A WINDWARD BOOK

Random House *New York*

*This book is dedicated to
Andrew and Elizabeth,
just because.*

Windward Books are published by Random House, Inc.
First Windward Silverback Edition, October 1972.
Originally published by Random House, Inc., in 1963.

ISBN: 0-394-82197-1

Library of Congress catalog card number: 63-9033

Manufactured in the United States of America

Contents

*Ghosts
and
More
Ghosts*

Footsteps Invisible

tHE NIGHT WAS DARK, and violent with storm. Rain beat down as if from an angry heaven, and beneath its force all the noises of a metropolis blended oddly, so that to Jorman they sounded like the muted grumble of the city itself.

He himself was comfortable enough, however. The little box-sized newsstand beside the subway entrance was tight against the rain.

The window that he kept open to hear prospective customers, take in change, and pass out papers let in a wet chill, but a tiny oil heater in one corner gave out a glow of warmth that beat it back.

A transistor radio shrilled sweetly, and Foxfire, his toy wire-haired terrier, snored at his feet.

Jorman reached up and switched the radio off. There were times when it gave him pleasure. But more often he preferred to listen to life itself, as it poured past his newsstand like a river.

Tonight, though, even Times Square was deserted to the storm gods. Jorman listened and could not hear a single footstep, though his inner time sense —re-enforced by a radio announcement a moment before—told him it was barely past midnight.

He lit a pipe and puffed contentedly.

After a moment he lifted his head. Footsteps were approaching: slow, measured, familiar footsteps. They paused in front of his stand, and he smiled.

"Hello, Clancy," he greeted the cop on the beat. "A nice night for ducks."

"If I only had web feet," the big officer grumbled, " 'twould suit me fine. You're a funny one, now, staying out so late on a night like this, and not a customer in sight."

"I like it." Jorman grinned. "Like to listen to the storm. Makes my imagination work."

"Mine, too," Clancy grunted. "But the only thing it can imagine is my own apartment, with a hot tub and a hot drink waitin'. Arrgh!"

He shook himself, and with a "good night" tramped onward.

Jorman heard the officer's footsteps diminish. There was silence for a while, save for the rush of the rain and the occasional splashing whir of a cab sloshing past. Then he heard more steps.

This time they came toward him from the side street, and he listened intently to them, head cocked a little to one side.

They were—he searched for the right word—well, odd. *Shuffle-shuffle,* as if made by large feet encased in sneakers, and that slid along the pavement for a few inches with each step. *Shuffle-shuffle—shuffle-shuffle,* they came toward him slowly, hesitantly, as if the walker were pausing every few feet to look about him.

Jorman wondered whether the approaching man could be a cripple. A club-foot, perhaps, dragging one foot with each step. For a moment he had the absurd thought that the sounds were made by four feet, not two; but he dismissed it with a smile and listened more closely.

The footprints were passing him now, and though the rain made it hard to distinguish clearly, he had the impression that each shuffling step was accompanied by a slight clicking noise.

As he was trying to hear more distinctly, Foxfire woke from his slumbers. Jorman felt the little dog move at his feet, then heard the animal growling deep in its chest. He reached down and found Foxfire huddled against his shoe, tail tucked under, hair bristling.

"Quiet, boy!" he whispered. "I'm trying to hear."

Foxfire quieted. Jorman held his muzzle and listened. The footsteps of the stranger had shuffled past him to the corner. There they paused, as if in indecision. Then they turned south on Seventh Avenue, and after a moment were engulfed in the storm noise.

Jorman released his hold on his dog and rubbed

his chin, wondering what there could have been about the pedestrian's scent to frighten Foxfire so.

For a moment Jorman sat very still, his pipe clenched in his hand. Then with a rush of relief he heard Clancy's returning steps. The cop came up and stopped, and Jorman did not wait for him to speak. He leaned out his little window.

"Clancy," he asked, trying to keep the excitement out of his voice, "what does that fellow look like down the block there—the one heading south on Seventh? He ought to be about in the middle of the block."

"Huh?" Clancy said. "I don't see any guy. Somebody snitch a paper?"

"No." Jorman shook his head. "I was just curious. You say there isn't anyone——"

"Not in sight," the cop told him. "Must have turned in some place. You and me have this town to ourselves tonight. Well, be good. I got to try some more doors."

He sloshed away, the rain pattering audibly off his broad, rubber-coated back, and Jorman settled back into his chair chuckling to himself. It was funny what tricks sounds played on you, especially in the rain.

He relit his dead pipe and was thinking of shutting up for the night when his last customer of the evening approached. This time he recognized the steps. It was a source of pride to him—and of revenue as well—that he could call all of his regulars by name if they came up when the street wasn't too crowded.

This one, though he didn't come often and had never come before at night, was easy. The step was a firm, decisive one. *Click*—that was the heel coming down—*slap*—that was the sole being planted firmly. *Click-slap*—the other foot. Simple. He could have distinguished it in a crowd.

"Good morning, Sir Andrew," Jorman said as the steps came up to his stand. "*Times?*"

"Thanks." It was a typically British voice that answered. "Know me, do you?"

"Oh, yes." Jorman grinned. It was usually a source of mystification to his customers that he knew their names. But names were not too hard to learn, if the owners of them lived or worked near by. "A bellboy from your hotel was buying a paper last time you stopped. When you'd gone on, he told me who you were."

"That easy, eh?" Sir Andrew Carraden exclaimed. "Don't know as I like it so much, though, being kept track of. Prefer to lose myself these days. Had enough of notoriety in the past."

"Had plenty of it four years ago, I suppose," Jorman suggested. "I followed the newspaper accounts of your tomb-hunting expedition. Interesting work, archaeology. Always wished I could poke around in the past that way, sometime."

"Don't!" The word was sharp. "Take my advice and stay snug and cozy in the present. The past is an uncomfortable place. Sometimes you peer into it and then spend the rest of your life trying to get away from it. And—— But I mustn't stop here chatting. Not in this storm. Here's your money. No, here on the counter . . ."

And then, as Jorman fumbled for and found the

coin, Sir Andrew Carraden exclaimed again.

"I say!" he said. "I'm sorry."

"Perfectly all right," Jorman told him. "It pleases me when people don't notice. A lot don't, you know, in spite of the sign."

"Blind newsdealer," Sir Andrew Carraden read the little placard tacked to the stand. "I say——"

"Wounded in the war," Jorman told him. "Sight failed progressively. Went entirely a couple of years ago. So I took up this. But I don't mind. Compensations, you know. Amazing what a lot a man can hear when he listens. But you're going to ask me how I knew you, aren't you? By your footsteps. They're very recognizable. Sort of a *click-slap, click-slap.*"

His customer was silent for a moment. Jorman was about to ask whether anything was wrong when the Englishman spoke.

"Look. I——" and his tone took on an almost hungry eagerness——"I've got to talk to somebody, or blow my top. I mean, go barmy. Completely mad. Maybe I am, already. I don't know. You—you might have a few minutes to spare? You might be willing to keep me company for an hour? I—it might not be too dull."

Jorman hesitated in answering. Not because he intended to refuse—the urgency in the man's voice was unmistakable—but there was something of a hunted tone in Sir Andrew Carraden's voice that aroused Jorman's curiosity.

It was absurd—but Jorman's ears were seldom wrong. The Englishman, the archaeologist whose name

had been so prominent a few years back, was a hunted
man. Perhaps a desperate man. A fugitive—from what?

Jorman did not try to guess. He nodded.

"I have time," he agreed.

He bent down and picked up Foxfire, attached the
leash, threw an old ulster over his shoulders, and
turned down his bright gasoline lantern. With Foxfire
straining at the leash, he swung up his racks and
padlocked the stand.

"This way," Sir Andrew Carraden said at his side.
"Not half a block. Like to take my arm?"

"Thanks." Jorman touched the other's elbow. The
touch told him what he remembered from photographs
in papers he had seen, years back. The Englishman
was a big man. Not the kind to fear anything. Yet
now he was afraid. In fact, he was very little short
of terrified.

They bowed their heads to the somewhat lessened
rain and walked the short distance to the hotel.

They turned into the lobby, their heels loud on
marble. Jorman knew the place: the Hotel Russet.
Respectable, but a bit run down.

As they passed the desk, a sleepy clerk called out.

"Oh, pardon me. There's a message here for you.
From the manager. Relative to some work we've been
doing——"

"Thanks, thanks," Jorman's companion answered im-
patiently, and Jorman heard paper stuffed into a
pocket. "Here's the elevator. Step up just a bit."

They had been seated in easy chairs for some
minutes, pipes going, hot drinks in front of them, be-

fore Sir Andrew Carraden made any further reference
to the thing that was obviously on his mind.

The room they were in was fairly spacious, judging
from the reverberations of their voices, and since it
seemed to be a sitting room, probably was joined to a
bedroom beyond. Foxfire slumbering at Jorman's feet,
they had been talking of inconsequentials when the
Englishman interrupted himself abruptly.

"Jorman," he said, "I'm a desperate man. I'm being
hunted."

Jorman heard coffee splash as an unsteady hand let
the cup rattle against the saucer.

"I guessed so," he confessed. "It was in your voice.
The police?"

Sir Andrew Carraden laughed, a harsh, explosive
sound.

"Your ears *are* sharp," he said. "The police? I wish
it were! No. By a—a personal enemy."

"Then couldn't the police——" Jorman began. The
other cut him short.

"No! They can't help me. Nobody in this world
can help me. And God have mercy on me, nobody
in the next!"

Jorman passed over the emphatic exclamation.

"But surely——"

"Take my word for it, I'm on my own," Sir Andrew
Carraden told him, his voice grim. "This is a—a feud,
you might say. And I'm the hunted one. I've done a
lot of hunting in my day, and now I know the other
side of it. It's not pleasant."

Jorman sipped at his drink.

"You—this enemy. He's been after you long?"

"Three years." The Englishman's voice was low, a bit unsteady. In his mind Jorman could see the big man leaning forward, arm braced against knee, face set in grim lines.

"It began one night in London. A rainy night like this. I was running over some clay tablets that were waiting deciphering. Part of the loot from the tomb of Tut-Ankh-Tothet. The one the stories in the papers you referred to were about.

"I'd been working pretty hard. I knocked off for a pipe and stood at the window looking out. Then I heard it."

"Heard it?"

"Heard him." Carraden corrected himself. "Heard *him* hunting for me. Heard his footsteps——"

"Footsteps?"

"Yes. In the pitch-black night. Heard him tramping back and forth as he tried to locate me. Then he picked up my trail and came up the garden path."

Sir Andrew paused, and Jorman heard the coffee cup being raised again.

"My dog, a great Dane, scented him. He was frightened, poor beast, and with reason. But he tried to attack. My—enemy—tore the dog to pieces on my own doorstep. I couldn't see the fight, but I could hear. The beast held him up long enough for me to run for it. Out the back door, into the storm.

"There was a stream half a mile away. I made for that, plunged into it, floated two miles down, went ashore, picked up a ride to London. Next morning I left London on a freighter for Australia before he could pick up my trail again."

Jorman heard the archaeologist draw a deep breath.

"It took him six months to get on to me again, up in the Australian gold country. Again I heard him in time. I got away on a horse as he was forcing his way into my cabin, caught a cargo plane for Melbourne, took a fast boat to Shanghai. But I didn't stay there long."

"Why not?" Jorman asked. He fancied that Carraden had shuddered slightly.

"Too much like his own country. Conditions were—favorable for him in the Orient. Unfavorable for me. I had a hunch. I hurried on to Manila and took a plane for the States there. Got a letter later from an old Chinese servant that *he* arrived the next night."

Jorman sipped slowly at his coffee, his brow knitted. He did not doubt the man's sincerity, but the story *was* a bit puzzling.

"This fellow, this enemy of yours," he commented slowly, "you said the Orient was too much like his own country. I assume you mean Egypt."

"Yes. He comes from Egypt. I incurred his—well, his enmity there."

"He's a native then? An Egyptian?"

Carraden hesitated, seeming to choose his words.

"Well, yes," he said finally. "In a way you might call him a native of Egypt. Though, strictly speaking, he comes from another—another country. One less well known."

"But," Jorman persisted, "I should think that you,

a man of wealth, would have all kinds of recourse against a native, no matter where he might be from. After all, the man is bound to be conspicuous, and ought to be easy to pick up. I know you said the police could not help you, but have you tried? And how in the world does the fellow follow you so persistently? From London to Australia to Shanghai— that's a thin trail to run down."

"I know you're puzzled," the other told him. "But take my word for it, the police are no good. This chap—well, he just isn't conspicuous, that's all. He moves mostly by night. But even so he can go anywhere.

"He has—well, methods. And as for following me, he has his own ways of doing that, too. He's persistent. So awfully, awfully persistent. That's the horror of it: that blind, stubborn persistence with which he keeps on my trail."

Jorman was silent. Then he shook his head.

"I admit you've got me curious," he told Carraden. "I can see easily enough there are some things you don't want to tell me. I suppose the reason he's hunting you so doggedly is one of them."

"Right," the Englishman admitted. "It was while the expedition was digging out old Tut-Ankh-Tothet. It was something I did. A law I violated. A law I was aware of, but—well, I went ahead anyway.

"You see, there were some things we found buried with old Tothet the press didn't hear of. Some papyri, some clay tablets. And off the main tomb a smaller one . . .

"Well, I can't tell you more. I violated an ancient law, then got panicky and tried to escape the consequences. In doing so, I ran afoul of this—this fellow. And brought him down on my neck. If you don't mind——"

There was a desperate note in his host's voice. Jorman nodded.

"Certainly," he agreed. "I'll drop the subject. After all, it's your business. You've never tried to ambush the fellow and have it out with him, I suppose?"

He imagined Carraden shaking his head.

"No use," the other said shortly. "My only safety is in flight. So I've kept running. When I got to 'Frisco, I thought I was safe for a while. But this time he was on my heels almost at once. I heard him coming up the street for me late one foggy night. I got out the back door and ran for it. Got away to the Canadian plains.

"I planted myself out in the middle of nowhere, on a great, rolling grassy plain with no neighbor for miles. Where no one would even think of me, much less speak to me or utter my name. I was safe there almost a year. But in the end it was—well, almost a mistake."

Carraden put down his cup with a clatter. Jorman imagined it was because the cup had almost slipped from shaking fingers.

"You see, out there on the prairie there were no footsteps. This time he came at night, as usual, and he was almost on me before I was aware of it. And my horse was lame. I got away. But it was a near thing. Nearer than I like to remember . . .

"So I came to New York. I've been here since, in the very heart of the city. It's the best place of all to hide. Among people. So many millions crossing and recrossing my path muddy up the trail, confuse the scent——"

"Confuse the scent?" Jorman exclaimed.

Carraden coughed. "Said more than I meant to, that time," he admitted. "Yes, it's true. He scents me out. In part, at least. It's hard to explain. Call it the intangible evidences of my passage."

"I see." The man's voice pleaded so for belief that Jorman nodded, though he was far from seeing.

"I've been here almost a year now," the Englishman told him. "Almost twelve months with no sign of him. I've been cautious; man, how cautious I've been! Lying in my burrow like a terrified rabbit.

"Most of that time I've been right here, close to Times Square, where a million people a day cut my trail. I've huddled in my two rooms here—there's a bedroom beyond—going out only by day. He is usually most active at night. In the day people confuse him. It's the lonely reaches of the late night hours he likes best. And it's during them I huddle here, listening wakefully . . .

"Except on stormy nights like this. Storms make his job more difficult. The rain washes away my scent, the confusion of the winds and the raging of the elements dissipate my more intangible trail. That's why I ventured out tonight.

"Some day, even here, he'll find me," Sir Andrew

Carraden continued, his voice tight with strain. "I'm prepared. I'll hear him coming—I hope—and as he forces this door, I'll get out through the other one, the one in the bedroom, and get away. I early learned the folly of holing up in a burrow with only one exit. Now I always have at least one emergency doorway.

"Believe me, man, it's a ghastly existence. The lying awake in the quiet hours of the night, listening, listening for him; the clutch at the heart, the sitting bolt upright, the constant and continuing terror——"

Carraden did not finish his sentence. He was silent for several minutes, fighting, Jorman imagined, for self-control. Then the springs of his easy chair squeaked as he leaned forward.

"Look," the Englishman said then, in such desperate earnestness that his voice trembled a bit. "You must wonder whether I just brought you up here to tell you this tale. I didn't. I had a purpose. I told you the story to see how you reacted. And I'm satisfied. Anyway, you didn't openly disbelieve me; and if you think I'm crazy, maybe you'll humor me anyway. I have a proposition to make."

Jorman sat up a bit straighter. "Yes?" he asked, his face expressing uncertainty. "What——"

"What kind of proposition?" Carraden finished the sentence for him. "This. That you help me out by listening for him."

Jorman jerked his head up involuntarily, so that if he had not been blind he would have been staring into the other's face.

"Listen for your enemy?"

"Yes," the Englishman told him, voice hoarse. "Listen for his approach. Like a sentinel. An outpost. Look, man, you're down there in your little stand every evening from six on, I've noticed. You stay until late at night. You're posted there not fifty yards from this hotel.

"When he comes, he'll go by you. He's bound to have to cast about a bit, to unravel the trail—double back and forth like a hunting dog, you know, until he gets it straightened out.

"He may go by three or four times before he's sure. You have a keen ear. If he goes by while you're on the job, you're bound to hear him."

Carraden's voice quickened, became desperately persuasive.

"And if you do, you can let me know. I'll instruct the doorman to come over if you signal. Or you can leave your stand and come up here; you can make it easily enough, only fifty paces. But somehow you must warn me. Say you will, man!"

Jorman hesitated in his answer. Sir Andrew mistook his silence.

"If you're frightened," he said, "there's no need to be. He won't attack you. Only me."

"That part's all right," Jorman told him honestly. "What you've told me isn't altogether clear, and—I'll be frank—I'm not absolutely sure whether you're sane or not. But I wouldn't mind listening for you. Only, don't you see, I wouldn't have any way of recognizing your enemy's step."

Carraden gave a little whistling sigh that he checked at once.

"Good man!" The exclamation was quiet, but his voice showed relief. "Just so you'll do it. That last bit is easy enough. I've heard him several times. I can imitate his step for you, I think. There's only one thing worrying me.

"He—not everyone can hear him. But I'm counting on your blindness to give your ears the extra sensitivity—— No matter. We have to have a go at it. Give me a moment."

Jorman sat in silence and waited. The rain, beating against the panes of two windows, was distinctly lessening. Somewhere distant a fire siren wailed a banshee sound.

Carraden was making a few tentative scrapings, with his hands or his feet, on the floor.

"Got it!" he announced. "I've put a bedroom slipper on each hand. It's a noise like this."

With the soft-soled slippers, he made a noise like the shuffle of a large bare foot—a double sound, *shuffle-shuffle*, followed by a pause, then repeated.

"If you're extra keen," he announced, "you can hear a faint click or scratch of claws at each step. But——"

Then Jorman heard him sit up straight, knew Carraden was staring at his face.

"What is it, man?" the Englishman cried in alarm. "What's wrong?"

Jorman sat very tense, his fingers gripping the arms of his chair.

"Sir Andrew," he whispered, his lips stiff, "Sir Andrew! I've already heard those footsteps. An hour ago in the rain he went by my stand."

In the long silence that followed, Jorman could guess how the blood was draining from the other man's face, how the knuckles of his hands clenched.

"Tonight?" Carraden asked then, his voice harsh and so low that Jorman could hardly hear him. "Tonight, man?"

"Just a few minutes before you came by," Jorman blurted. "I heard footsteps—*his* steps—shuffling by. The dog woke up and whimpered. They approached me slowly, pausing, then going on."

The Englishman breathed. "Go on, man! What then?"

"They turned. He went down Seventh Avenue, going south."

Sir Andrew Carraden leaped to his feet, paced across the room, wheeled, came back.

"He's tracked me down at last!" he said in a tight voice, from which a note of hysteria was not far absent. "I've got to go. Tonight. Now. You say he turned south?"

Jorman nodded.

"But that means nothing," Carraden spoke swiftly, as if thinking out loud. "He'll find he's lost the track. He'll turn back. And since he passed, I've made a fresh trail. The rain may not have washed it quite away. He may have picked it up. He may be coming up those stairs now. Where's my bag? My passport? My money? All in my bureau. Excuse me. Sit tight."

Jorman heard a door flung open, heard the man rush

into the adjoining bedroom, heard a tight bureau drawer squeal.

Then Carraden's footsteps again. A moment later, a bolt on a door was pulled back. Then the door itself rattled. A pause, and it rattled again, urgently. Once again, this time violently. Jorman could hear Carraden's loud breathing in the silence that followed.

"The door won't open!" There was an edge of fear in the Englishman's voice as he called out. "There's a key or something in the lock. From the outside."

He came back into the sitting room with a rush, paused beside Jorman.

"That message!" The words came through Carraden's teeth. "The one the clerk handed me. I wonder if——"

Paper ripped, rattled. Sir Andrew Carraden began to curse.

"The fool!" he almost sobbed. "Oh, the blasted, blasted fool. 'Dear sir' "—Carraden's voice was shaking now—" 'redecoration of the corridor on the north side of your suite necessitated our opening your door this afternoon to facilitate the painting of it. In closing and locking it, a key inadvertently jammed in the lock, and we could not at once extricate it. Our locksmith will repair your lock promptly in the morning. Trusting you will not be inconvenienced——'

"Heaven deliver us from fools!" Sir Andrew gasped. "Luckily there's still time to get out this way. Come on, man, don't sit there. I'll show you down. But we must hurry, hurry."

Jorman heard the other man's teeth chattering faintly

together in the excess of emotion that was shaking him,
felt the muscular quivering of near-panic in the big
man as he put out his hand and took Sir Andrew's
arm to help himself rise. And then, as he was about
to lift himself, his fingers clamped tight about the
Englishman's wrist.

"Carraden!" he whispered. "Carraden! *Listen!*"

The other asked no question. Jorman felt the quivering muscles beneath his fingers tense. And a silence
that was like a hand squeezing them breathless seemed
to envelop the room. There was not even the faint,
distant sound of traffic to break it.

Then they both heard it. In the hallway, coming
toward the door. The faint padding sound of shuffling
footsteps . . .

It was Foxfire, whimpering piteously at their feet,
that broke the spell momentarily holding them.

"He——" Carraden's word was a gasp——"he's out
there!"

He left Jorman's side. Jorman heard him shoving
with desperate strength at something heavy. Castors
squeaked. Some piece of furniture tipped over and
fell with a crash against the inside of the door.

"There!" Carraden groaned. "The desk. And the
door's bolted. That'll hold him a moment. Sit tight,
man. Hold the pup. He'll ignore you. It's me he
wants. I've got to get that other door open before
he can come through."

His footsteps raced away into the bedroom. Jorman
sat where he was, Foxfire under his arm, so tense
that his muscles ached from sheer fright.

In the bedroom there was a crash, as of a man plunging against a closed door that stubbornly would not give. But above the noise from the bedroom, Jorman could hear the barricaded door—the door beyond which *he* was—start to give.

Nails screamed as they came forth from wood. Hinges groaned. And the whole mass—door, lintels, desk—moved inward an inch or so. A pause, and then the terrible, inexorable pressure from the other side came again. With a vast rending the door gave way and crashed inward over the barricading furniture.

And in the echoes of the crash Jorman heard the *shuffle-shuffle* of feet crossing the room toward the bedroom.

In the bedroom Sir Andrew Carraden's efforts to force the jammed door ceased suddenly. Then the Englishman screamed, an animal cry of pure terror from which all intelligence was gone. The window in the bedroom crashed up with a violence that shattered the glass.

After that there was silence for a moment, until Jorman's acute hearing caught, from the street outside and five floors down, the sound of an object striking the pavement.

Sir Andrew Carraden had jumped . . .

Somehow Jorman found the strength to stumble to his feet. He dashed toward the door, and fell over the wreckage of it. Hurt, but not feeling it, he scrambled up again and stumbled into the hall and down the corridor.

Somehow his questing hands found a door that was

sheathed in metal, and he thrust it open. Beyond were bannisters. Stairs. By the sense of feel he made his way down.

How many minutes it took to reach the lobby, to feel his way blindly past the startled desk clerk out to the street, he did not know. Or whether he had gotton down before *he* had—the totally inhuman thing that had been hunting Sir Andrew Carraden.

Once outside on the wet pavement, cool night air on his cheek, he paused, his breath coming in sobbing gasps. And as he stood there, footsteps, shuffling footsteps, passed close by him from behind and turned westward.

Then Jorman heard an astounding thing. He heard Sir Andrew Carraden's footsteps also, a dozen yards distant, hurrying away from him.

Sir Andrew Carraden had leaped five floors. And still could walk . . .

No, run. For the tempo of the man's steps was increasing. He was trotting now. Now running. And behind the running footsteps of Carraden were *his* steps, the enemy's, moving more swiftly, too, something scratching loudly on the concrete each time he brought a foot down. Something that might be claws . . .

"Sir Andrew!" Jorman called loudly, senselessly. "Sir An——"

Then he stumbled and almost fell, trying to follow. Behind him the desk clerk came hurrying up. He exclaimed something in shocked tones, but Jorman did not even hear him. He was bending down, his hand exploring the object over which he had stumbled.

"Listen!" Jorman gasped to the desk clerk, jittering above him. "Tell me quickly! I have to know. What did the—the man look like who followed me out of the hotel just now?"

"F-followed you?" the clerk stuttered. "Nobody f-followed you. Not a soul. Nobody but you has gone in or out in the last hu-half hour. Listen, why did he do it? Why did he jump?"

Jorman did not answer him.

"Dear heaven," he was whispering, and in a way it was a prayer. "Oh, dear heaven!"

His hand was touching the dead body of Andrew Carraden, lying broken on the pavement.

But his ears still heard those footsteps of pursued and pursuer, far down the block, racing away until not even he could make them out any longer. The hunted still fleeing, the invisible hunter still following, even beyond the boundaries of death. . . .

Mr. Milton's Gift

tHIS STORY is going to answer a question you've probably asked yourself a hundred times. And you'll see, when you've finished, that it's just about the only possible answer, even though some of the things I'm going to tell you may sound a little surprising at first.

The fellow I'm going to tell you about is Homer Milton, who was thirty-three when all this happened: a nice, quiet chap who minded his own business and had been married for eight years to a very pretty wife named Martha, whom he loved very much. Homer was a bookkeeper, and his boss, Mr. Springer, was a tough egg who often kept him working late.

This particular night Mr. Springer had kept him even later than usual, and it was Martha's birthday, which is how Homer happened to step into Ye Olde Giftte Shoppe to buy her a present. Homer had never

noticed Ye Olde Giftte Shoppe before, but this particular night he was walking home from the office by
a different route and there it was, with a vacant lot
on one side and a warehouse on the other.

The place was dark, except for a faint yellow light
that gleamed through the dusty window, just bright
enough to show up the words painted on the glass,
Ye Olde Giftte Shoppe. It certainly wasn't much of
a place, even for a "giftte shoppe." But here he was,
almost home, with Martha expecting a nice birthday
present and every other store in the neighborhood shut
tight, so—well, Homer stepped through the doorway.

As soon as he was inside, though, he concluded
he'd made a mistake. Inside, the place looked even
less like a giftte shoppe and more like a junkke shoppe.

In one corner was what looked like an egg the size
of a bushel basket, and hanging from the ceiling above
it was a pair of old slippers with little wings at the
heels. Homer could have sworn he saw the wings beat
a couple of times, but of course it was just a trick of
the shadows caused by the old oil lamp hanging from
the ceiling.

There was more, but he couldn't quite make out
what the rest of the stock consisted of, for it was
covered with a fine assortment of cobwebs. He'd seen
enough, though, to make him decide to take his trade
elsewhere, when he heard the clearing of a throat
behind him.

Homer spun around. There beside a long dusty
counter stood the proprietor, looking at Homer. He
couldn't have been more than four feet tall—his eyes

were on a level with Homer's middle coat button. Very
curious eyes they were, too—large and round and
glowing yellow, like a jack-o'-lantern's—and set in a
pointed face made to seem even smaller by two ears
uncommonly long and sharp.

"Good evening, Mr. Milton," the fellow said, very
pleasantly. The yellow jack-o'-lantern eyes blinked
once, and the pointed tip of one ear twitched. "Can
I do anything for you?"

"Uh," Homer mumbled, "I was just looking for a
gift for my wife. But I don't see anything suitable."
And he started backing toward the door.

He didn't make it, though. One long thin arm shot
out—seeming to stretch as if made of rubber—and
caught him by the coat and pulled him back.

"Now, sir!" The strange proprietor cocked his head
at Homer, the large yellow eyes glowing. "A gift for
your wife? Exactly! Is she the nagging kind? Is she
extravagant, talkative, greedy? Or have you just grown
tired of her for no reason, which often happens?"

"Why—why, no," Homer stammered. "It's nothing
like that at all."

"No matter," the little fellow said, rubbing his hands
with a dry, whisking sound. "Your reasons are your
own. Whatever you want, we have it. Antimony, spirits
of hemlock, silken nooses, henbane—which do you prefer? If you'll let me make a suggestion, I advise you
to take my own special Spirit-away Powder. Just dust
it lightly over a sleeping wife and experience no
further annoyance."

"Why, I don't want any of those things!" Homer

said indignantly. "I love my wife. She does worry too much about making me wear rubbers in wet weather, and she cries if I forget her birthday or our anniversary, but outside of that I haven't any complaint."

"Extraordinary!" The yellow eyes blinked twice. "Can't recall when a husband has said such a thing to me in centuries. I must think."

This he did, resting a sharp chin in one hand and closing his eyes for several seconds. Then he beamed at Homer.

"To be sure," he said. "You want to give your wife something as an evidence of your affection. A natural mistake on my part. I usually sell such gifts only for brides. So now: What kind of gift did you have in mind?"

"Why, just a gift," Homer said. "Something to show her I love her, and to keep her satisfied so I can get the work done I'm taking home tonight. I was thinking of a silver cream pitcher."

"A silver cream pitcher! My dear sir, I don't deal in such articles! You said you wanted a gift, didn't you? Well, that's what I sell here—gifts. Now come, come, give me some notion what gift your wife would like. What does she seem to desire most in life, or feel the absence of most keenly? By the way, call me Clarence. That's my name."

"Why—er—Mr. Clarence," Homer Milton mumbled, considerably bewildered by now, "what she wants most, I guess, is for me to make more money. I'm not very good at asking for raises, and Mr. Springer is a very hard man to talk to, so——"

"The gift of making money!" Clarence rubbed his hands together. "Now we're progressing. That would be a gift she'd appreciate, eh? If you had the gift of making money?"

"Why, yes," Homer agreed. "But that would be a gift I'd have to have and—— Wait a minute, I'm getting all confused. We started out talking about one kind of gift and now we're talking about another. A birthday gift and the gift of making money aren't the same thing at all."

"Tut, tut," Clarence said. "A gift is a gift. We deal only in one kind here—the genuine article. Of course if you had the gift of making money, it would be a gift your wife would appreciate for her birthday."

"But——" By now Homer's head was spinning. "How could I explain to Martha that I had a gift for making money, which was a birthday gift for her, because—— Oh, dear," he groaned. "I don't feel well. I have to go. Really I do. I'll come back some other time."

Clarence's hand darted out again and seized his lapel.

"Nonsense!" the little man said. "Have you ten dollars?"

"Yes," Homer gulped, "but——"

"Then it's a deal. Grasp my hand firmly." He thrust out a long thin hand, curiously cool and dry to the touch, and Homer took it. He couldn't help himself.

"Shillings, pounds and pence, dollars, dimes and cents," Clarence chanted, his eyes closed. "By this hand may you make 'em, even if you have to fake 'em. Abracadabra and so forth."

The yellow eyes opened.

"There," the little man said. "It's done. Spell enough for an easy gift like that one. Ten dollars, please."

In a daze Homer took out his wallet and handed over the money.

"Now," Clarence said, "you're entitled to our free gift offer, extra-special this year only—one gift free with every gift you buy. Hold out your hand again."

Homer tried to refuse, but Clarence grabbed it anyway.

"June, moon, love, dove, sigh, die," he chanted, eyes tight shut. "You're a poet, you will know it. Abracadabra, et cetera."

Opening his eyes, he beamed at Homer.

"There!" he said. "Now you have the gift of verse too. Only appropriate gift I could think of to match your name. Homer and Milton! Great fellows, both of them. Great poets, too. Well, I'm certainly happy you came in. Haven't had a customer in I don't know how long, and I was almost ready to shut up shop and move somewhere else. Come in any time you want another gift. I have the finest stock in this hemisphere. The gift of gab, of music, of courage, of second sight, of optimism, of punctuality—all those and lots more. See you again, Mr. Milton."

He gave a quick, bobbing bow and a moment later Homer found himself out in the street once more, wondering confusedly how Clarence had known his name.

It was three blocks farther on before Homer was anything like himself again. He decided against trying to get his ten dollars back—no telling what might happen if he tangled with Clarence and Ye Olde Giftte Shoppe again. One thing was certain, though—he'd have to keep the whole affair secret from Martha.

And he still had to find her a present, too.

Well, he didn't have any trouble with the present, as it turned out. There was a second-hand shop only a block from his apartment and he caught the proprietor just as he was closing up. Homer bought a silver cream pitcher that the fellow had polished so you couldn't tell it had been used at all. They were both a bit startled when Homer said, "I want a present for my wife, a silver pitcher or a knife," but then they grinned and assumed he had accidentally made a rhyme.

Homer began to wonder a little, though, when he got home and handed Martha the pitcher and said tenderly, "Just a present for my dear one, hope it doesn't seem a queer one. It's nothing fancy, it is true, but it shows that I love you."

Martha gaped at him and, flabbergasted, he gaped back. But then Martha laughed happily and patted his cheek.

"What a silly you are!" she said. "Even making up a verse to go with it. It makes me very happy that you didn't forget what the day is. And I've cooked a special dinner for you—roast beef, mashed potatoes and peas, with ice cream for dessert."

"That sounds like a dandy dinner, though not the

kind to make me thinner," Homer said with enthusiasm. "Mashed potatoes and roast beef please me 'most beyond belief; I will probably stuff and stuff. Are you sure you have enough?"

Martha gave him a strange look.

"Homer, you're certainly talking very oddly. Even if it's just a joke, I wish you'd stop it."

"Certainly, dear, if it'll please you," Homer mumbled, unfolding his paper and plumping himself down behind it in his easy chair. "I was only trying to tease you."

Then, rather than risk any more conversation, he devoted himself to the sports page. But his mind was not on American League standings.

His mind was back in Ye Olde Giftte Shoppe. And a horrible suspicion was coming over him that Clarence, the odd little proprietor——

But it wasn't possible! It simply wasn't!

"It isn't true!" Homer muttered to himself. "It isn't true. Such things can't be done to you!" Then, realizing he had spoken in verse again, he shut up. Maybe it wasn't true, but just the same——

Dinner was a strained affair. Martha kept glancing at him strangely, and for his part Homer confined his conversation to monosyllables. By the time dinner was over Martha was almost in tears. She pointedly put the silver cream pitcher out of sight, and when she had finished the dishes she went off to bed without even saying good night.

Unhappily, Homer got out the ledgers he'd brought home with him and tried to work on them. He uncapped the beautiful Swiss-made fountain pen Martha

had given him for a wedding present, the one that
wrote in black, green, blue or red. He had never seen
another one like it in this country and with it in his
fingers his work was usually a pleasure. But not tonight. His mind kept wandering.

He found himself with Martha's scissors in his hand,
aimlessly clipping a sheet of notepaper into rectangles.
Sternly he focused his mind again on the ledgers—
but his mind wouldn't stay there. He kept thinking
of Ye Olde Giftte Shoppe and Clarence and wondering if——

But the more he thought about the evening's strange
happenings, the more bewildered he became. His
thoughts kept chasing themselves around like mice
playing tag. Then he came to himself with a start
and realized he'd been sitting there no telling how
long, woolgathering and doodling with his fountain pen
all over one of the slips of paper he'd cut out. He
might as well be in bed.

Breakfast the next morning did not start the day
off on quite the right note, though Homer came to
the table ready to apologize.

"Good morning, my dear; the day seems clear," he
said. "Coffee smells swell, hope you slept well. I
believe I'll decide to have my eggs fried."

The beginnings of a smile fled from his wife's clear,
youthful features. Her lips closed tightly and a single
tear, squeezing from the corner of her eye, was her
only answer.

Homer finished his toast and coffee, skipped the eggs,
grabbed his hat and briefcase, and marched toward

the door. Then he turned, as always, to kiss Martha good-by.

"Homer," she said then, "do you think you should go off to the office today? I mean—perhaps you're ill. Maybe you should go see Dr. Phelps. I thought you were just teasing me, but——"

"I am not even slightly ill; I have no need to take a pill," Homer said with dignity. "If I've caused you any pain, I'm sorry—but I can't explain. Now excuse me, but I'm late. Mr. Springer hates to wait. I really have to go to work; my job you know I never shirk."

Then, as the tears welled up in Martha's clear blue eyes again, he hastily closed the door. It was terrible, worrying her like this, but suppose he tried to tell her the truth? Then she'd be positive he was going out of his mind, and she'd worry twice as much. . . .

Homer tried to forget his troubles by plunging into work as soon as he reached the office. But he'd barely opened his ledgers when the phone rang. It was Martha.

"Homer!" she said tenderly over the telephone. "You darling! Oh, I'm so ashamed of being angry at you. But what a funny way to give me such a wonderful present."

"What did you say?" Homer asked, baffled. "Repeat it, pray."

"I said you're a darling, leaving it on the sideboard for me to find after you'd left, and making me realize how bad-tempered I'd been, and how good to me you really were. Now I can't talk any more—I'm hurrying right downtown."

She hung up and Homer, rubbing his forehead, put the phone down. He couldn't imagine what she was talking about, but he didn't have time to think about it now because there was work to be done on the books and Mr. Springer would want to see them as soon as he came in. So Homer plunged into his work. Luck was with him this time. The figures balanced easily, and Mr. Springer didn't show up until almost noon. By then Homer had the books finished and was sitting back, daydreaming and doodling with his fountain pen. He was thinking—suppose some day he did acquire the gift of making money and got rich? First thing he'd do would be to take Martha on a second honeymoon, a trip around the world, and then——

"Milton!"

Homer jumped. It was Mr. Springer himself, standing by his chair, looking down, his fishlike face very red.

"I've been calling you for the last five minutes!"

"Sorry, Mr. Springer, didn't mean to linger," Homer mumbled and gathered up the books. Mr. Springer stalked into his private office and Homer followed. Then for several minutes he just sat while Mr. Springer, grunting occasionally, leafed through the ledgers. Presently Mr. Springer stopped at an item.

"This three-thousand-dollar rebate for Willis and Company," he growled. "What was that for?"

"That one's easy to explain, it was just a damage claim," Homer said without thinking. "Freight car in a wreck, smashed our shipment all to heck. We paid Willis, railroad paid us; no one made a bit of fuss."

"What?" Mr. Springer's jaw had dropped. "Milton, what's wrong with you? Are you sick?"

"No, sir," Homer gulped and closed his mouth before he could say anything that rhymed.

"Well, you're talking very oddly!"

He continued with the ledgers, looking suspiciously at Homer from the corners of his eyes from time to time. At last he came to the final page.

"All right, Milton," he began; then his jaw dropped even lower than before. He was staring goggle-eyed at something on the final page. Nervously Homer peered over to see what it was.

It was a hundred-dollar bill, pasted to the bottom of the ledger sheet.

No, not pasted. Drawn there! Just one side of it, of course, the side with Benjamin Franklin's portrait on it. But it certainly looked real.

Mr. Springer's eyes popped. First he tried to pick up the hundred. Then he ran his fingers over it and found it really was drawn on the page.

"Milton, what does this mean?" he thundered.

Homer swallowed hard. Now he remembered doodling something while daydreaming about being rich—he must have drawn the bill then. It was a perfect hundred-dollar bill, right down to the last fine pen-strokes—only he'd drawn it with a fountain pen on a page of a ledger!

"I don't know, I'm quite sure," Homer stammered. "I know it wasn't there before."

What Springer would have said to this he never

knew. At that instant the office door burst open and
Miss Perkins, the receptionist, stood there looking
scared.

"Mr. Springer, there's two men here want to see
Mr. Milton, and——"

But the men hadn't waited. They came right in,
big men, solid men, with hard eyes and square jaws.

"Treasury Department," the first one said. "We want
to talk to Homer Milton. His wife's just been picked
up for passing a phony hundred-dollar bill and she says
he gave it to her."

"Is that so?" Mr. Springer said. "There's your man.
I always thought he had a criminal face. Now excuse
me. I have to call my auditors and order a complete
check of his accounts."

So in practically no time Homer was in the pokey,
his mind a whirl of dismay and bewilderment. Of
course they didn't haul him right down and toss him
heave-ho through the jail doors. First they took him
to a big, gloomy building, and there was Martha,
red-eyed and sobbing.

"Oh, Homer," she wailed, "why did you do it? I
told you I wanted nice things but I didn't want them
so badly you had to become a counterfeiter. I was
happy, really, I was!" And she began to sob again.

After that the hard-eyed, square-jawed men ques-
tioned him, first one, then another. But the more
Homer tried to explain about Clarence and Ye Olde
Giftte Shoppe, with those jingly verses coming out
every time he opened his mouth—well, you can

imagine the results.

"We've got hold of a whack!" one of the men finally said wearily. "There's no such place as this Olde Giftte Shoppe in the directory, and our men can't find any such establishment in that neighborhood. Put him in a cell and give him twenty-four hours to think it over; then we'll question him again. Those awful rhymes are driving me crazy!"

They let Martha have one final word with him before they dragged him away.

"It's all my fault, darling; you did it for me," she said sobbingly, clinging to him and taking the press out of his coat with her tears. "I don't care what you've done, I love you and I'll stand by you. My sister's husband's cousin is Mortimer Flugle the criminal lawyer, and I'm going to hire him for you right away."

This evidence of Martha's love and affection cheered Homer up for a little while, but when he found himself alone in a cold cell, his spirits began to droop again. He was in a bad spot, and he knew it.

Last night he'd been doodling with his fountain pen on a slip of paper—only he hadn't just been doodling. Unknown to him, his hand was drawing a perfect hundred-dollar bill.

Then later in the office he'd been daydreaming and doodling again, and this time his hand had drawn one side of a hundred-dollar bill on Mr. Springer's ledgers. All because of that silly charm Clarence had recited last night in Ye Olde Giftte Shoppe, " 'Shillings, pounds and pence, dollars, dimes and cents; by this hand may you make 'em, even if you have to fake 'em.' "

"Hey, Milton!" called the guard. "You got a visitor.
Here's your mouthpiece. Ten minutes, Counselor."

The cell door opened and closed and Homer looked
up at Mortimer Flugle, his wife's sister's husband's
cousin. Mortimer Flugle was large and paunchy, with
a chin that had been doubled and redoubled, and a
pink face adorned by glasses on a black ribbon. He
didn't just exude benevolence, he broadcast it.

"Well, well, Milton," said Flugle. "Charged with
counterfeiting, eh? Mighty good workmanship too, I
hear. Suppose you tell me about it."

Homer shrugged dolefully.

"I bought a gift for making money; the gift would
really be a honey if the money wasn't funny." He
sighed. "I mean phony. I mean——"

He stopped. Flugle was staring at him oddly.

"You're upset," the lawyer said soothingly. "Suppose
you start over and try again."

Homer took a deep breath.

"I tried to buy my wife a present, something she'd
consider pleasant. I didn't want her to be vexed, so
I wound up getting hexed. A gift this Clarence fellow
sold me, but the thing he never told me was I'd be a
counterfeiter——"

He stopped again, for Mortimer Flugle had backed
away.

"It's all right, Milton, perfectly all right," Flugle said.
"Naturally you're upset. I'll tell you what. Now as I
understand it you claim you drew that phony century

note with your fountain pen. Suppose you just demonstrate for me, so I'll know how strong their case is.
I've brought you some paper cut to the right size
and——"

At Homer's look he stopped.

"Yes, yes, of course," Flugle burbled, backed right
up against the cell door. "Then let's do it this way:
You write down all the facts instead, while I go chat
with the boys. I'll be back in half an hour or so and
we'll map our strategy."

He pressed some paper into Homer's hand, called
the guard, and left hurriedly. Homer didn't blame him.
He took out his fountain pen. But what was the use
of writing anything? Who would believe the truth?
And what else could he tell them? All he could do
was plead guilty and go off to Atlanta or Leavenworth
—or maybe Alcatraz. And perhaps while he was in
prison the hex would wear off.

Homer had already served half his sentence, in his
mind, when the cell door reopened and Flugle came
in again.

"Well, well, got it all written out?" Flugle asked,
taking the oblong pad from Homer. "Now let's just
see——"

He stopped with a strangled noise that sounded like
"*Awrk!*" He held up the pad and stared at it. Then
he lowered it and stared at Homer.

"So it's true!" he breathed. "You said you had a gift,
my boy—but it's more than a gift, it's sheer genius."

"What?" Homer asked. "What are you talking about,
Flugle? Or are you just blowing, like a bugle?"

Flugle ignored the insult.

"This, my boy," he said. "I'm talking about this."
He held up the pad, and Homer turned slightly green.
While he was daydreaming he had turned one of those
precut slips of paper into another hundred-dollar bill!

He snatched for it, but Flugle put the pad in his
pocket.

"Now, Milton, calm yourself," he crooned. "I'm not
going to mention this to anybody. Instead I'm going
right up and bail you out myself, even if the bail is
twenty-five thousand dollars. We must have a con-
ference about this gift of yours, Milton; we really
must!"

That is how it happened that an hour later Homer
Milton was driving across town with Flugle himself
at the wheel, a gleam in his eye that Homer didn't like.

"Now, Milton," Flugle said, "I'm not going to ask
you how you do it. How, with an ordinary fountain
pen, you can whip up a bill that could fool the Treasury men, is your secret. But you have a gift—no, a
genius—and it must be properly harnessed.

"The thing that tripped you up was the paper. Now
it just happens that I have another client who has also
had a little trouble with the authorities. But in his
case it wasn't the paper, it was the engraving that
stopped him.

"So it occurred to me, why shouldn't I introduce you
to each other? He has a fine stock of paper and you
—well, you have the ability to make that paper worth
something. What you and he do in a business way
after I've introduced you is no concern of mine. But

I predict you'll both do extraordinarily well, and I hope you won't forget it was Mortimer Flugle who brought you together.

"As for the present little trouble of yours, I've already got three different lines of defense mapped out, and there's always insanity to fall back on. If we need that, all we have to do is put you on the stand and let you start your story about that little fellow you call Clarence, and it's in the bag."

He put a large, soft hand reassuringly on Homer's arm, but the truth is Homer wasn't listening. For they were driving down a dingy, badly lit street near his apartment and all of a sudden he saw a shop that looked familiar. As they came abreast of it he saw he was right. There were the words on the window, Ye Olde Giftte Shoppe, and a single light inside, just barely visible.

"Flugle!" Milton shouted. "There's the shop, so come to a stop! Step on the brake, you legal fake!"

"What?" Flustered, Flugle brought the car to a stop. "What's the matter, Milton?"

But Homer did not pause to bandy words with him —or verses. He opened the door and leaped to the sidewalk.

"Milton!" Flugle wailed. "Come back here. I put up your bail out of my own pocket!"

But by then Homer was halfway down the block. He reached Ye Olde Giftte Shoppe and hurled himself through the door.

"Clarence!" He skidded to a stop in the dusty gloom of the interior. "Show your face or else I'll start to take this place of yours apart! To you I dearly want to speak, so away don't try to sneak!"

Two jack-o'-lantern eyes popped up from behind the counter and blinked at him, separately.

"Good evening," Clarence said, the pointed tip of his right ear twitching twice. "Why, it's Mr. Milton! Come to buy another gift? Dear me, just when I was closing up my shop and moving to another location, too."

"No!" cried Homer. "I want you just to take them back! I can live with money's lack, but free me from this dreadful curse of talking thus in awful verse and penning counterfeited money. The fix I'm now in isn't funny!"

"I'm sorry," Clarence said firmly, "but I can't do it. All sales are final. If I didn't make that rule, people would be forever trying to get their money back. You know how people are, never satisfied."

Well, at that Homer got even more excited and he almost exploded, trying to explain to Clarence that he didn't want his money, he just wanted to give back the gifts. All the explanations came out in those jingling verses until Homer almost screamed from sheer frustration. And in his excitement he said some things he shouldn't have, because Clarence drew himself up to his full four feet and told Homer he couldn't take back any goods, he was closing up shop and there wasn't room in the crates for a single item more.

"I'm going to try the sixteenth century this time," Clarence said. "They'll have more faith in my merchandise. Nobody believes in me in this century of yours—nobody but you, and even you aren't satisfied. Now good-by, Mr. Milton!"

Homer looked around and saw it was true—the shop was empty except for several big packing-cases already nailed up and one Clarence was just getting ready to close. He started to put the lid on and at that Homer became more desperate than ever. He began to beg and plead in such heart-rending verses that at last Clarence weakened.

"All right," he said. "Just to be obliging I'll exchange one of the gifts for any other gift you choose. But I can't exchange them both and I can't take them back. It's impossible. This is my first sale in goodness knows when and if I check in at the home office without even one sale on my books, I may not get another chance. So that's the best deal I can make and I'm stretching things to do it. Now which gift do you want to return —and what do you want in exchange for it?"

Homer didn't even have to think. He said he'd keep the gift of verse and turn in the gift of making money—because no matter what people thought, they couldn't put you in jail for talking in rhyme. Then he named the gift he'd take in exchange. So Clarence took his hand and mumbled:

"Dibbery dobbery, flummery flobbery; even exchange is no robbery."

"There," he said, "it's all done. And don't worry about what happened today. Now that the gift's gone, the evidence is gone too. Well, good-by, Mr. Milton."

With that, Clarence put the lid into place on the last crate and hammered it down. And with the last

hammer blow Clarence and the crates vanished and
Homer Milton found himself standing alone in an
empty, dusty store. Even the lettering, Ye Olde Giftte
Shoppe, was gone from the window.

When Homer's case came up for trial, there wasn't
any evidence against him—just a blank piece of paper
nobody would believe had once been a counterfeit
hundred-dollar bill.

So the judge let him go, though he gave him a very
stern talking-to first, to which Homer answered not a
word. In fact, from the moment he stepped out of
Ye Olde Giftte Shoppe that second time he scarcely
opened his mouth except to eat. No matter what was
said to him, he just smiled and didn't answer.

He's never been in any trouble since, and you may
even know him—a very nice-looking chap in his late
thirties, going just a little bald, with an extremely attractive wife who does all the talking when they're
out together. The reason for that is because there in
Ye Olde Giftte Shoppe, when he realized he had to
keep the gift of verse he chose the gift of silence, too.

So the two pretty well even each other out except
at home, where Martha has got quite used to hearing
Homer comment on the day's news in couplets and
quatrains. And in fact, listening to Homer discuss the
Giants' chances for the pennant is as good as hearing
someone recite "Casey at the Bat."

Martha would be quite upset if Homer ever changed,
because she soon saw where his talents could be put
to a commercial use. So she didn't let him go back
to bookkeeping. She steered him into a new line and

now Homer is just about a millionaire.

You know all those thousands of greeting cards that are sold for Mother's Day and Father's Day and Christmas and birthdays and anniversaries and just about every other day? You must have asked yourself a hundred times where they get all the inane verses on those cards. Well, here's the answer:

Eighty percent of them are written by Homer Milton.

Next time you get one, read the verse out loud. You're almost sure to recognize his style.

The Rose-Crystal Bell

TWENTY YEARS had left no trace inside Sam Kee's little shop on Mott Street. There were the same dusty jars of ginseng root and tigers' whiskers, the same little bronze Buddhas, the same gimcracks mixed with fine jade. Edith Williams gave a little murmur of pleasure as the door shut behind her and her husband.

"Mark," she said, "it hasn't changed! It doesn't look as if a thing had been sold since we were here on our honeymoon."

"It certainly doesn't," Dr. Mark Williams agreed, moving down the narrow aisle behind her. "If someone hadn't told us Sam Kee was dead, I'd believe we'd stepped back twenty years in time, as they do in those scientific stories young David reads."

"We must buy something," his wife said. "For a twentieth anniversary present for me. Perhaps a bell?"

From the shadowy depths of the shop a young man emerged, American in dress and manner despite the Oriental contours of his face and eyes.

"Good evening," he said. "May I show you something?"

"We think we want a bell." Dr. Williams chuckled. "But we aren't quite sure. You're Sam Kee's son?"

"Sam Kee, junior. My honored father passed to the halls of his ancestors five years ago. I could just say that he died——" black eyes twinkled—— "but customers like the more flowery mode of speech. They think it's quaint."

"I think it's just nice, and not quaint at all," Edith Williams declared. "We're sorry your father is dead. We'd hoped to see him again. Twenty years ago when we were a very broke young couple on a honeymoon he sold us a wonderful rose-crystal necklace for half price."

"I'm sure he still made a profit." The black eyes twinkled again. "But if you'd like a bell, here are small temple bells, camel bells, dinner bells . . ."

But even as he spoke, Edith Williams's hand darted to something at the back of the shelf.

"A bell carved out of crystal!" she exclaimed. "And rose-crystal at that. What could be more perfect? A rose-crystal wedding present and a rose-crystal anniversary present!"

The young man half stretched out his hand.

"I don't think you want that," he said. "It's broken."

"Broken?" Edith Williams rubbed off the dust and held the lovely bell-shape of crystal, the size of a pear, to the light. "It looks perfect to me."

"I mean it is not complete." Something of the American had vanished from the young man. "It has no clapper. It will not ring."

"Why, that's right." Mark Williams took the bell. "The clapper's missing."

"We can have another clapper made," his wife declared. "That is, if the original can't be found?"

The young Chinese shook his head.

"The bell and the clapper were deliberately separated by my father twenty years ago." He hesitated, then added: "My father was afraid of this bell."

"Afraid of it?" Mark Williams raised his eyebrows. The other hesitated again.

"It will probably sound like a story for tourists," he said. "But my father believed it. This bell was supposedly stolen from the temple of a sect of Buddhists somewhere in the mountains of China's interior. Just as many Occidentals believe that the Christian Judgment Day will be heralded by a blast on St. Peter's trumpet, so this small sect is said to believe that when a bell like this one is rung, a bell carved from a single piece of rose crystal, and consecrated by ceremonies lasting ten years, any dead within sound of it will rise and live again."

"Heavenly!" Edith Williams cried. "And no pun intended. Mark, think what a help this bell will be in your practice when we make it ring again!" To the Chinese she added, smiling: "I'm just teasing him. My husband is really a very fine surgeon."

The other bowed his head.

"I must tell you," he said, "you will not be able to make it ring. Only the original clapper, carved from the same block of rose crystal, will ring it. That is why my father separated them."

Again he hesitated.

"I have told you only half of what my father told me. He said that, though it defeats death, Death cannot be defeated. Robbed of his chosen victim, he takes another in his place. Thus when the bell was used in the temple of its origin—let us say when a high priest or a chief had died—a slave or servant was placed handy for Death to take when he had been forced to relinquish his grasp upon the important one."

He smiled, shook his head.

"There," he said. "A preposterous story. Now if you wish it, the bell is ten dollars. Plus, of course, sales tax."

"The story alone is worth more," Dr. Williams declared. "I think we'd better have it sent, hadn't we, Edith? It'll be safer in the mail than in our suitcase."

"Sent?" His wife seemed to come out of some deep feminine meditation. "Oh, of course. And as for its not ringing—I shall make it ring. I know I shall."

"If the story is true," Mark Williams murmured, "I hope not. . . ."

The package came on a Saturday morning, when Mark Williams was catching up on the latest medical publications in his untidy, book-lined study. He heard Edith unwrapping paper in the hall outside. Then she came in with the rose-crystal bell in her hands.

"Mark, it's here!" she said. "Now to make it ring."

She plumped herself down beside his desk. He took the bell and reached for a silver pencil.

"Just for the sake of curiosity," he remarked, "and not because I believe that delightful sales talk we were given, let's see if it will ring when I tap. It should, you know."

He tapped the lip of the bell. A muted *thunk* was the only response. Then he tried with a coin, a paper knife, and the bottom of a glass. In each instance the resulting sound was nothing like a bell ringing.

"If you've finished, Mark," Edith said then, with feminine tolerance, "let me show you how it's done."

"Gladly," her husband agreed. She took the bell and turned away for a moment. Then she shook the bell vigorously. A clear, sweet ringing trembled through the room—so thin and ethereal that small involuntary shivers crawled up her husband's spine.

"Good Lord!" he exclaimed. "How did you do that?"

"I just put the clapper back in place with some thread," Edith told him.

"The clapper?" He struck his forehead with his palm. "Don't tell me—the crystal necklace we bought twenty years ago!"

"Of course." Her tone was composed. "As soon as young Sam Kee told us about his father's separating the clapper and the bell, I remembered the central crystal pendant on my necklace. It *is* shaped like a bell clapper—we mentioned it once.

"I guessed right away we had the missing clapper. But I didn't say so. I wanted to score on you, Mark——" she smiled affectionately at him—— "and because, you know, I had a queer feeling Sam Kee, junior, wouldn't let us have the bell if he guessed we had the clapper."

"I don't think he would have." Mark Williams picked up his pipe and rubbed the bowl with his thumb. "Yet he didn't really believe that story he told us any more than we do."

"No, but his father did. And if old Sam Kee had told it to us—remember how wrinkled and wise he seemed?—I'm sure we'd have believed the story."

"You're probably right." Dr. Williams rang the bell and waited. The thin, sweet sound seemed to hang in the air a long moment, then was gone.

"Nope," he said. "Nothing happened. Although, of course, that may be because there was no deceased around to respond."

"I'm not sure I feel like joking about the story." A small frown gathered on Edith's forehead. "I had planned to use the bell as a dinner bell and to tell the story to our guests. But now—I'm not sure."

Frowning, she stared at the bell until the ringing of the telephone in the hall brought her out of her abstraction.

"Sit still, I'll answer." She hurried out. Dr. Williams, turning the rose crystal bell over in his hand, could hear the sudden tension in her voice as she answered. He was on his feet when she re-entered.

"An emergency operation at the hospital." She sighed. "Nice young man—automobile accident. Fracture of the skull, Dr. Amos says. He wouldn't have disturbed you but you're the only brain man in town, with Dr. Hendryx away on vacation."

"I know." Mark Williams was already in the hall, reaching for his hat. "Man's work is from sun to sun, but a doctor's work is never done," he misquoted.

"I'll drive you," Edith followed him out. "You sit back and relax for another ten minutes. . . ."

Mark Williams drew off his rubber gloves with a weary sense of failure. He had lost patients before, but never without a feeling of personal defeat. Edith said he put too much of himself into every operation. Perhaps he did. And yet—— But there was no reason for the boy to have died. Despite his injury his condition at the beginning of the operation had been excellent.

But in the middle of it he had begun to fail, his respiration to falter, his pulse to become feeble. And just as Mark Williams was completing his delicate stitching, he had ceased to breathe.

Why? Mark Williams asked himself. But there was probably no answer. Life was a flukey and unpredictable thing. Take the other lad he had operated on the night before. He had been in far worse shape than this one, and had come through with flying colors. In Room 9, just across the hall, he was gathering strength for another fifty years of life.

Young Dr. Amos, who had been the anesthetist, came over and clapped him understandingly on the shoulder as he reached for his suit coat.

"Too bad, Mark," he said. "Nobody could have done a finer job. Life just didn't want that lad, I'm afraid."

"Thanks, John." Mark tried to sound cheerful. "That's how it is, sometimes. I'd rather like an autopsy, just to satisfy myself."

"Of course. I'll order it. You look a bit tired. Go on home. Here, let me help you with your coat."

Mark Williams slid into the jacket and, when he tried to button it, became aware of the bulky object in one pocket.

"Now what's this?" he asked, and fished out the rose-crystal bell, which he had undoubtedly thrust into his pocket when the telephone call had come. "Edith's bell! She won't thank me for carrying it around this way. . . ."

"Mark, catch it!" young Amos cried as the crystal object slipped through Dr. Williams's weary fingers. It was Amos himself who caught it, a flying catch in midair that rescued the bell before it could smash on the floor. The bell tinkled abruptly, a thin, high sound, then rested silently in Amos's palm.

"That was a close one!" the younger man said. "Pretty thing. What is it?"

"A Chinese dinner bell," Mark Williams answered. "I'd better——" He didn't finish. Behind them Nurse Wythe was calling excitedly.

"Doctor! Doctor Williams! The patient's respiration is beginning! His pulse is beating. Come quickly!"

"What?" He whirled and strode back to the operating table. It was true. Pulse and respiration had re-established themselves. Even as he stood there both were gaining in strength.

"Good Lord!" breathed young Amos. "Now isn't that

something! Spontaneous re-establishment of life! I never read of anything quite like this, Mark. I think we're going to save him after all."

They had saved him, quite definitely, when Nurse McGregor slipped into the operating room.

"I'm sorry to bother you, Doctor Williams," she said, in great agitation. "But could you come to the patient in Nine at once? He was doing splendidly, but five minutes ago he had a sudden relapse. I left Nurse Johnson with him and came for you—but I'm afraid he's dead."

It was lucky that traffic was light as they drove homeward. More than once Mark found himself to the left of the center line and had to pull back.

"Now why did that boy die?" he demanded. "Why, Edith? . . . By the way, here's that rose-crystal bell. Better put it in your handbag . . . He was doing fine. And then, just as we were saving one boy we thought we'd lost—we lost the one we thought we'd saved."

"These things happen, darling," she said. "You know that. A doctor can only do so much. Some of the job always remains in the hands of Nature. And she does play tricks at times."

"Yes, confound it, I know it," her husband growled. "But I resent losing that lad. There was no valid reason for it—unless there was some complication I overlooked." He shook his head, scowling. "I ordered an autopsy but—— Yes, I'm going to do that autopsy myself. I'm going to turn back and do it now. I want to know!"

He pulled abruptly to the left to swing into a side road and turn. Edith Williams never saw the car that hit them. She heard the frantic blare of a horn and a scream of brakes, and in a frozen instant realized that there had been someone behind them, about to pass. Then the impact came, throwing her forward into the windshield and unconsciousness.

Edith Williams opened her eyes. Even before she realized that she was lying on the ground and that the figure bending over her was a State Trooper, she remembered the crash. Her head hurt but there was no confusion in her mind. Automatically, even as she tried to sit up, she accepted the fact that there had been a crash, help had come, and she must have been unconscious for several minutes at least.

"Hey, lady, take it easy!" the Trooper protested. "You had a bad bump. You got to lie still until the ambulance gets here. It'll be along in five minutes."

"Mark," Edith said, paying no attention. "My husband! Is he all right?"

"Now, lady, please. He's being taken care of. You——"

But she was not listening. Holding on to the State Trooper's arm, she pulled herself to a sitting position. She saw the car on its side some yards away, other cars pulled up, a little knot of staring people. Saw them and dismissed them. Her gaze found her husband, lying on the ground a few feet away, a coat folded beneath his head.

Mark was dead. She had been a doctor's wife for

twenty years, and before that a nurse. She knew death when she saw it.

"Mark." The word was spoken to herself, but the Trooper took it for a question.

"Yes, lady," he said. "He's dead. He was still breathing when I got here, but he died two, three minutes ago."

She got to her knees. Her only thought was to reach his side. She scrambled across the few feet of ground to him still on her knees and crouched beside him, fumbling for his pulse. There was none. There was nothing. Just a man who had been alive and now was dead.

Behind her she heard a voice raised. She turned. A large, disheveled man was standing beside the Trooper, talking loudly.

"Now listen, officer," he was saying, "I'm telling you again, it wasn't my fault. The guy pulled sharp left right in front of me. Not a thing I could do. It's a wonder we weren't all three of us killed. You can see by the marks on their car it wasn't my fault——"

Edith Williams closed her mind to the voice. She let Mark's hand lie in her lap as she fumbled in her bag, which she somehow still clutched in her fingers. She groped for a handkerchief to stem the tears which would not be held back. Something was in the way— something smooth and hard and cold. She drew it out and heard the thin, sweet tinkle of the crystal bell.

The hand in her lap moved. She gasped and bent forward as her husband's eyes opened.

"Mark!" she whispered. "Mark, darling!"

"Edith," Mark Williams said with an effort. "Sorry—— darned careless of me. Thinking of the hospital . . ."

"You're alive!" she said. "You're *alive!* Oh, darling, darling, lie still, the ambulance will be here any second."

"Ambulance?" he protested. "I'm all right now. Help me sit up."

"But Mark——"

"Just a bump on the head." He struggled to sit up. The State Trooper came over.

"Easy, buddy, easy," he said, his voice awed. "We thought you were gone. Now let's not lose you a second time."

"Hey, I'm sure glad you're all right!" the red-faced man said in a rush of words. "Whew, fellow, you had me all upset, even though it wasn't my fault. I mean, how's a guy gonna keep from hitting you when—when——"

"Catch him!" Mark Williams cried, but the trooper was too late. The other man plunged forward to the ground and lay where he had fallen without quivering.

The clock in the hall struck two with muted strokes. Cautiously Edith Williams rose on her elbow and looked down at her husband's face. His eyes opened and looked back at her.

"You're awake," she said, unnecessarily.

"I woke up a few minutes ago," he answered. "I've been lying here—thinking."

"I'll get you another sedative pill. Dr. Amos said

for you to take them and sleep until tomorrow."

"I know. I'll take one presently. You know—hearing that clock just now reminded me of something."

"Yes?"

"Just before I came to this afternoon, after the crash, I had a strange impression of hearing a bell ring. It sounded so loud in my ears I opened my eyes to see where it was."

"A—bell?"

"Yes. Just auditory hallucination, of course."

"But, Mark——"

"Yes?"

"A—a bell did ring. I mean, I had the crystal bell in my bag and it tinkled a little. Do you suppose——"

"Of course not." But though he spoke swiftly he did not sound convincing. "This was a loud bell. Like a great gong."

"But—I mean, Mark darling—a moment earlier you —had no pulse."

"No pulse?"

"And you weren't breathing. Then the crystal bell tinkled and you—you . . ."

"Nonsense! I know what you're thinking and believe me—it's nonsense!"

"But Mark." She spoke carefully. "The driver of the other car. You had no sooner regained consciousness than he——"

"He had a fractured skull!" Dr. Williams interrupted sharply. "The ambulance intern diagnosed it. Skull fractures often fail to show themselves and then— bingo, you keel over. That's what happened. Now let's say no more about it."

"Of course." In the hall, the clock struck the quarter hour. "Shall I fix the sedative now?"

"Yes—no. Is David home?"

She hesitated. "No, he hasn't got back yet."

"Has he phoned? He knows he's supposed to be in by midnight at the latest."

"No, he—hasn't phoned. But there's a school dance tonight."

"That's no excuse for not phoning. He has the old car, hasn't he?"

"Yes. You gave him the keys this morning, remember?"

"All the more reason he should phone." Dr. Williams lay silent a moment. "Two o'clock is too late for a 17-year-old boy to be out."

"I'll speak to him. He won't do it again. Now please, Mark, let me get you the sedative. I'll stay up until David——"

The ringing phone, a clamor in the darkness, interrupted her. Mark Williams reached for it. The extension was beside his bed.

"Hello," he said. And then, although she could not hear the answering voice, she felt him stiffen. And she knew. As well as if she could hear the words she knew, with a mother's instinct for disaster.

"Yes," Dr. Williams said. "Yes . . . I see . . . I understand . . . I'll come at once . . . Thank you for calling."

He slid out of bed before she could stop him.

"An emergency call." He spoke quietly. "I have to go." He began to throw on his clothes.

"It's David," she said. "Isn't it?" She sat up. "Don't try to keep me from knowing. It's about David."

"Yes," he said. His voice was very tired. "David is hurt. I have to go to him. An accident."

"He's dead." She said it steadily. "David's dead, isn't he, Mark?"

He came over and sat beside her and put his arms around her.

"Edith," he said. "Edith—— Yes, he's dead. Forty minutes ago. The car went over a curve. They have him—at the County morgue. They want me to—identify him. Identify him, Edith! You see, the car caught fire!"

"I'm coming with you," she said. "I'm coming with you!"

The taxi waited in a pool of darkness between two street lights. The long, low building which was the County morgue, a blue lamp over its door, stood below the street level. A flight of concrete steps went down to it from the sidewalk. Ten minutes before, Dr. Mark Williams had gone down those steps. Now he climbed back up them, stiffly, wearily, like an old man.

Edith was waiting in the taxi, sitting forward on the edge of the seat, hands clenched. As he reached the last step she opened the door and stepped out.

"Mark," she asked shakily, "was it——"

"Yes, it's David." His voice was a monotone. "Our son. I've completed the formalities. Now the only thing we can do is go home."

"I'm going to him!" She tried to pass. He caught her wrist. Discreetly the taxi driver pretended to doze.

"No, Edith! There's no need. You mustn't see him!"

"He's my son!" she cried. "Let me go!"

"No! What have you got under your coat?"

"It's the bell, the rose-crystal bell!" she cried. "I'm going to ring it where David can hear!"

Defiantly she brought forth her hand, clutching the little bell. "It brought you back, Mark! Now it's going to bring back David!"

"Edith!" he said in horror. "You mustn't believe that's possible. You can't. Those were coincidences. Now let me have it."

"No! I'm going to ring it." Violently she tried to break out of his grip. "I want David back! I'm going to ring the bell!"

She got her hand free. The crystal bell rang in the quiet of the early morning with an eerie thinness, penetrating the silence like a silver knife.

"There!" Edith Williams panted. "I've rung it. I know you don't believe, but I do. It'll bring David back." She raised her voice. "David!" she called. "David, son! Can you hear me?"

"Edith," Dr. Williams groaned. "You're just tormenting yourself. Come home. Please come home."

"Not until David has come back . . . David, David, can you hear me?" She rang the bell again, rang it until Dr. Williams seized it, then she let him take it.

"Edith, Edith," he groaned. "If only you had let me come alone . . ."

"Mark, listen!"

"What?"

"Listen!" she whispered with fierce urgency.

He was silent. And then fingers of horror drew themselves down his spine at the clear, youthful voice that came up to them from the darkness below.

"Mother? . . . Dad? . . . Where are you?"

"David!" Edith Williams breathed. "It's David! Let me go! I must go to him."

"No, Edith!" her husband whispered frantically, as the voice below called again.

"Dad? . . . Mother? . . . Are you up there? Wait for me."

"Let me go!" she sobbed. "David, we're here! We're up here, son!"

"Edith!" Mark Williams gasped. "If you've ever loved me, listen to me. You mustn't go down there. David— I had to identify him by his class ring and his wallet. He was burned—terribly burned!"

"I'm going to him!" She wrenched herself free and sped for the steps, up which now was coming a tall form, a shadow shrouded in the darkness.

Dr. Williams, horror knotting his stomach, leaped to stop her. But he slipped and fell headlong on the pavement, so that she was able to race panting down the stairs to meet the upcoming figure.

"Oh, David," she sobbed, "David!"

"Hey, Mom!" The boy held her steady. "I'm sorry. I'm terribly sorry. But I didn't know what had happened until I got home and you weren't there and then one of the fellows from the fraternity called me. I realized they must have made a mistake, and you'd come here, and I called for a taxi and came out here. My taxi let me off at the entrance around the block, and I've been looking for you down there . . . Poor Pete!"

"Pete?" she asked.

"Pete Friedburg. He was driving the old car. I lent him the keys and my driver's license. I shouldn't have—but he's older and he kept begging me. . . ."

"Then—then it's Pete who was killed?" she gasped. "Pete who was—burned?"

"Yes, Pete. I feel terrible about lending him the car. But he was supposed to be a good driver. And then their calling you, you and Dad thinking it was me——"

"Then Mark was right. Of course he was right." She was laughing and sobbing now. "It's just a bell, a pretty little bell, that's all."

"Bell? I don't follow you, Mom."

"Never mind," Edith Williams gasped. "It's just a bell. It hasn't any powers over life and death. It doesn't bring back and it doesn't take away. But let's get back up to your father. He may be thinking that the bell—that the bell really worked."

They climbed the rest of the steps. Dr. Mark Williams still lay where he had fallen headlong on the pavement. The cab driver was bending over him, but there was nothing to be done. The crystal bell had been beneath him when he fell, and it had broken. One long, fine splinter of crystal was embedded in his heart.

The Marvelous Stamps from El Dorado

NOW THESE TRIANGULARS," Malcolm said proudly, pointing to a glass frame behind which were five stamps in faded shades of red, blue, green, yellow and black, "make up probably the rarest and most interesting complete set known to philatelists. Their value is not definitely established, since they've never been sold as a unit. But——"

It was at this point that Morks interrupted. Malcolm had gotten further in his narration than was usual, with Morks around. But Morks—his full name is Murchison Morks—had been bending forward to peer at the stamps, and it took him a moment to straighten and turn.

"They are certainly rare," Morks said in that modest, melancholy way of his, "but I once had a set of stamps that were even rarer, and more interesting."

Malcolm's face took on a dark tinge of displeasure. Morks did not appear to notice it. If my morning paper ever tells of the finding of a body of an unidentified man of about forty, hair sandy, face long and sad, whose death resulted from a violent beating, I shall know that Morks has met his destined fate.

For, no matter what you may have seen, Morks has seen something stranger. Whatever you have done, he has done something more thrilling. Wherever you have been, he has been there before you, and under circumstances of considerably more danger.

And whatever you may own, he has owned something rarer.

The fate reserved for men like Morks is brutal in the extreme. For years their fellows put up with them, permit interruptions by them, listen to them, and grit their teeth. But at last someone's self-control is bound to snap.

And when that day comes, all who knew him will shake their heads but admit the deed to have been quite justified.

I am surprised that I myself have not been the instrument of judgment upon Morks before this. Heaven knows that I have suffered . . .

But I started to recount the tale Morks told in response to the jog Malcolm's remark had given his memory—or his imagination.

That is the insidious thing about Morks. No matter how he may exasperate you, you listen. And when he has finished, though you may disbelieve his story utterly you cannot possibly prove it is not true.

And sometimes days later you find yourself muttering aloud, uttering objections you could not think of at the time that might have broken Morks down into admitting he was lying. Without, yourself, even yet being entirely *positive* . . .

But there I go again. I must restrain myself, for I at least have devised a way of getting even.

I take Morks's stories down and, when they are not too fantastic, sell them. In this way I recoup the sums Morks sponges from me in the form of cash and meals. (The lodging I give him from time to time, on the couch in my study, I do not assess against him. That costs me nothing.)

So, as to the stamps:

"You own a set *rarer* than my triangulars?" Malcolm asked; and the dark blood was creeping higher into his cheeks.

But Morks was quite oblivious to Malcolm's raised tones, which had attracted the notice of all the other members in the room.

Malcolm's valuable stamp collection was on exhibit there as a feature of a forthcoming visitors' day at our club—the one day of the year when the club's portals open to the members' women relatives and their friends.

"Not own, no." Morks shook his head in gentle correction. "Owned."

"Oh!" Malcolm snorted. "I suppose they got burned? Or stolen? Or lost?"

"No—" and here Morks heaved a sigh—"I used them. For postage, I mean. Before I realized their utter uniqueness."

Malcolm gnawed at his lip.

"This set of stamps," he said, laying a hand on the glass covering the triangular bits of paper, "cost the life of at least one man."

"Mine," Morks replied instantly, his voice soft—as it always became, strangely, once he had attracted everyone's attention—"cost me my best friend."

"Cost you the *life* of your best friend?" Malcolm demanded, through tight-clenched teeth.

Morks shook his head, his face expressing a reflective sadness, as if in his mind he were living again a bit of the past that it still hurt him to remember.

"I don't know," he answered. "I really don't. I suspect not. I honestly think that Harry Norris—that was my friend—at this moment is a dozen times happier than any man here. And when I reflect that but for a bit of timidity on my part I might be with him——"

He broke off, seeing that all present had gathered within listening distance.

"But I had better tell you the whole story," he said more briskly, "so you can fully understand."

Smiling, as if pleased, Morks let himself drop into an easy chair, where he composed himself in comfort.

I am not a stamp collector myself (he began, with a pleasant nod toward Malcolm) but my father was. He died some years ago, and among other things he left me his collection.

It was not a particularly good one—he had leaned

more toward the picturesque in his items than toward
rarity or value—and when I sold it, I hardly got
enough for it to repay me for the trouble I went to
in having it appraised.

I even thought for a time of keeping it; for some
of his collection, particularly those stamps from tropical
countries that featured exotic birds and beasts, were
highly decorative.

But in the end I sold them all—except one set of
five which the dealer refused to take, because he said
they were forgeries.

Forgeries! If he had only guessed——

But naturally I took his word for it. I assumed he
knew. Especially since the five stamps differed considerably from any I had ever seen before, and had
not even been pasted into my father's album. Instead,
they had been loose in the envelope tucked in at the
rear of the book.

The dealer's view that they were forgeries gained
added credence from the fact that I could find no
space in the album where they might have been placed.
There was not even a section devoted to their country
—though this was not conclusive, since the album
was small and by no means included all the less-well-
known states.

But, forgeries or not, they were both interesting and
attractive. The five were in differing denominations:
ten cents, fifty cents, one dollar, three dollars, and
five dollars.

All were unused, in mint condition—that's the term,
isn't it, Malcolm?—and in the gayest of colors: vermil-

lion and ultramarine, emerald and yellow, orange and azure, chocolate and ivory, black and gold.

And since they were all large—their size was roughly four times that of the current airmail stamps—the scenes they showed had a vividness and reality lacking even in the most colorful of my father's other items.

In particular the three-dollar one, portraying the native girl with the platter of fruit on her head——

However, that's getting ahead of my story. Let me say simply that, thinking they were forgeries, I put them away in my desk and forgot about them for several years.

I found them again one night, quite by accident, when I was rummaging around in the back of a drawer. I was looking for an envelope in which to post a letter I had just written to my best friend, Harry Norris. Harry was at that time living in Boston; and as I found it impossible to leave New York, we kept up a frequent correspondence.

It so happened that the only envelope I could find was the one in which I had been keeping those stamps of my father's. I emptied them out, addressed the envelope, and then, after I had sealed the letter inside, found my attention attracted to those five strange stamps.

Their gaudy colors pleased the eye, and the pictures that graced them snared the imagination. As it was several years since I had put them away and forgotten them, many details concerning them had slipped my mind. Now I studied them more closely.

I have mentioned that they were all large and

rectangular: almost the size of baggage labels, rather
than of conventional postage stamps. But then, of
course, these were not conventional postage stamps.
Not in any sense of the word.

Across the top of them was a line in bold print:
Federated States of El Dorado. Then, on either
side, about the center, the denomination. And at the
bottom, another line, *Rapid Post.*

Being unfamiliar with such things, I had assumed
when first I found them that El Dorado was one of
those small Indian states, or perhaps that it was in
Central America. Rapid Post, I judged, would probably
correspond to our own airmail.

Since the denominations were in cents and dollars,
I rather leaned to the Latin America theory. There
are a lot of little countries down there that I'm always
getting confused, such as El Salvador and Colombia.
But until that moment I had never really given the
matter much thought.

Now, staring at them, I began to wonder whether
that dealer had known his business. They were done
so well, the engraving executed with such superb
verve, the colors so bold and attractive, that it hardly
seemed likely any forger could have gotten them up.
They looked like the real article to me.

It is true the subjects they depicted were far from
usual. The ten-cent value, for instance, pictured a
unicorn standing erect, head up, spiral horn pointing
skyward, mane flowing, the very breathing image of life.

It was almost impossible to look at it without
knowing that the artist had worked with a real unicorn

for a model. Except, of course, that there aren't any unicorns any more.

The fifty-center showed Neptune, trident held aloft, riding a pair of harnessed dolphins through a foaming surf. It was just as real as the first. The old boy even had a twinkle in his eye; and looking closely, you could make out that he was winking at a mermaid way off in the corner.

The one-dollar value depicted Pan playing on his pipes, with a Greek temple in the background, and three fauns dancing on the grass. Looking at it, I could almost hear the music he was making.

I'm not exaggerating in the least. I must admit I was a little puzzled that a tropical country should be putting Pan on one of its stamps, for I thought he was purely a Greek monopoly. But when I moved on to the three-dollar stamp, I forgot all about him.

I probably can't put into words quite the impression that stamp made upon me—and upon Harry Norris, later.

The central figure was a girl; I believe I spoke of that.

A native girl, against a background of tropical flowers, smiling a little secret smile that managed to combine the utter innocence of girlhood with all the inherited wisdom of a woman. On her head, native fashion, she was carrying a great flat platter piled high with fruit of every kind you can imagine.

I looked at her for quite a long time before I examined the last of the set—the five-dollar value.

This one was relatively uninteresting, by comparison

—just a map. It showed several small islands set down in an expanse of water labeled, in neat letters, *Sea of El Dorado*. I assumed that the islands represented the Federated States of El Dorado itself, and that the little dot on the largest, marked by the word Nirvana, was the capital of the country.

I quite forgot, for some minutes, about my letter to Harry Norris. I found myself thinking that, next time I took a boat trip, I really must arrange a stopover in El Dorado. Then my eye encountered the envelope and I recalled my original purpose.

Suddenly an idea occurred to me. Harry had a nephew who collected stamps. Just for the fun of it, I might put one of those El Dorado forgeries—if they were forgeries—on my letter to Harry, along with the regular stamp, and see whether it wouldn't go through the post office. If it did, Harry's nephew might get a rarity, a foreign stamp with an American cancellation, that might some day bob up to confound an expert.

It was a silly idea, but it was late at night and finding the stamps had put me in a gay mood. I promptly licked the ten-cent El Dorado, pasted it onto a corner of Harry's letter, and then got up to hunt a regulation stamp to put with it.

The search took me into my bedroom, where I found the necessary postage in the wallet I had left in my coat. While I was gone, I left the letter itself lying in plain sight on my desk.

But when I got back into the library, the letter was gone.

I don't need to say I was puzzled. There wasn't

any place it could have gone to. There wasn't anybody who could have taken it. The window was open, but it was a penthouse window overlooking twenty floors of empty space, and nobody had come in through it.

Nor was there any breeze that might have blown the envelope to the floor. I looked. In fact, I looked everywhere, growing steadily more puzzled.

And then, as I was about to give up in complete bafflement, my phone rang.

It was Harry Norris, calling me from Boston. His voice, as he said hello, was a little strained. I quickly found out why.

Three minutes before, as he was getting ready for bed, the letter I had just finished giving up for lost had come swooping in his window, and then fluttered to the floor at his feet.

The next afternoon, Harry Norris arrived in New York. I had promised him over the phone, after explaining about the El Dorado stamp on the letter, not to touch the others except to put them safely away until we could examine them together.

It was obvious that the stamp was responsible for what had happened. In some manner it had carried that letter from my library straight to Harry Norris's feet in an estimated time of three minutes, or at an average rate of approximately five thousand miles an hour.

It was a thought to stagger the imagination. Certainly it staggered mine.

Harry arrived just at lunch time, and over lunch I told him all I knew; just what I've told you now. He was disappointed at the meagreness of my information. But I couldn't add a thing to the facts we already knew, and those facts spoke for themselves.

Basically, they reduced to this: I had put the El Dorado stamp on Harry's letter, and promptly that letter had delivered itself to him with no intermediary processes whatever.

"No, that's not quite right!" Harry burst out. "Look, I brought the letter with me. And——"

He held it out to me, and I saw I had been wrong. There *had* been an intermediary process of some kind, for the stamp was canceled. Yes, and the envelope was postmarked, too, in a clearly legible, pale purple ink.

Federated States of El Dorado, the postmark said. It was circular, like our own; and in the center of the circle, where the time of cancellation usually is, was just the word *Thursday.*

"Today is Thursday," Harry remarked. "It was after midnight when you put the stamp on the letter?"

"Just after," I told him. "Seems queer these El Dorado people pay no attention to the hour and the minute, doesn't it?"

"Only proves they're a tropical country," Harry suggested. "Time means little or nothing in the tropics, you know. But what I was getting at is this. The Thursday postmark goes to show El Dorado is probably down in Central America, as you suggested. If it were in India, or the Orient, it would have been marked Wednesday, wouldn't it? On account of the time difference?"

"Or would it have been Friday?" I asked, rather doubtfully, not knowing much about those things. "In any case we can find out easily enough. We've just to look in the atlas. I don't know why I didn't think of it before."

Harry brightened.

"Of course," he said. "Where do you keep yours?"

But it turned out I hadn't any atlas in the house—not even a small one. So we phoned downtown to one of the big bookstores to send up their latest and largest atlas. And while we waited for it we examined the letter again and speculated upon the method by which it had been transmitted.

"Rapid Post!" Harry explained. "I should say so! It beats airmail all hollow. Why, if that letter actually went all the way to Central America, was canceled and postmarked, and *then* went on to Boston, its average speed must have been——"

We did a little rough calculation and hit upon two thousand miles a minute as a probable speed. When we'd done that, we looked at each other.

"Good Lord!" Harry gasped. "The Federated States of El Dorado may be a tropical country, but they've really hit upon something new in this thing! I wonder why we haven't heard about it before."

"They may be keeping it a secret," I suggested. "No, that won't do, because I've had the stamps for several years, and of course my father had them before that."

"I tell you, there's something queer here," Harry suggested, darkly. "Where are those others you told me about? I think we ought to make a few tests with them while we're waiting for that atlas."

With that I brought out the four remaining unused stamps, and handed them to him. Now Harry, among other things, was a rather good artist; and his whistle at the workmanship was appreciative. He examined each with care, but it was—I'd thought it would be— the three-dollar value that caught his eye.

"What a beauty!" Harry said aloud.

I didn't know whether he meant the stamp or the girl, but I had my suspicions. After all, that had been my own reaction; and Harry was younger than I. Also, I could add, a good bit handsomer.

Presently, however, Harry put that one aside and finished examining the others. Then he turned to me.

"The thing I can't get over," he commented, "is the *lifelikeness* of the figures. You know what I'd suspect if I didn't know better? I'd suspect these stamps were never engraved at all. I'd believe that the plates they came from were prepared by one of the new electric processes from photographs."

"From photographs!" I exclaimed; and Harry nodded.

"Of course, you know and I know they can't have been," he added. "Unicorns and Neptunes and Pans aren't running around to be photographed these days. But that's the feeling they give me."

I confessed that I had had the same feeling. But since we both agreed on the impossibility of its being so, we dismissed that phase of the matter and went back again to the problem of the method used in transporting the letter.

"You say you were out of the room when it vanished," Harry remarked. "That means you didn't see it go. You don't actually know what happened when you put that stamp on and turned your back, do you?"

I agreed that was so, and Harry sat in thoughtful silence for some moments, tapping his fingernails against his white, even teeth.

At last he looked up.

"I think," he said, "we ought to find out by using one of these other stamps to mail something with."

Why that hadn't occurred to me before I can't imagine. As soon as Harry said it, I recognized the rightness of the idea. The only thing was to decide what to send, and to whom.

That held us up for several minutes. There wasn't anybody else either of us cared to have know about this just yet; and we couldn't send anything to each other very well, being both there together.

"I'll tell you!" Harry exclaimed at last. "We'll send something to El Dorado itself!"

The thought excited him.

I agreed to that readily enough, but how it came about that we decided to send, not a letter, but Thomas à Becket, my aged and ailing Siamese cat, I can't remember.

All I know is that Harry suggested it, and it seemed logical enough at the time. Perhaps already there was beginning to stir in his mind an idea—— But as I say, I don't know. However it may have come about, Thomas à Becket we decided to send.

I do know that I told myself it would be a kind way

to dispose of the creature. Transmission through space at the terrific velocity of one hundred and twenty thousand miles an hour would surely put him out of his sufferings, quickly and painlessly. I would be saved the pangs of doing it myself, or having it done; and he, if he had any thoughts about it at all, could solace himself by the reflection that he had served a useful scientific end.

As to what the post office in El Dorado would think, finding itself the possessor of a defunct Siamese tomcat, I didn't speculate.

Thomas à Becket was asleep under the couch, breathing asthmatically and with difficulty. I found a cardboard box the right size and we punched some air holes in it. Then I gathered up Thomas and placed him in the container. He opened rheumy old eyes, gazed at me vaguely, and relapsed into slumber again. With a pang I put the lid on and we tied the box with heavy twine.

"Now," Harry said thoughtfully, "there's the question of how to address him, of course. However, any address will do for our purpose."

He took up a pen and wrote with rapidity. *Mr. Henry Smith, 711 Elysian Fields Avenue, Nirvana, Federated States of El Dorado.* And beneath that he added, *Perishable! Handle With Care!*

"But——" I began. Harry cut me off.

"No," he said, "of course I don't know of any such address. I just made it up. But the post office people won't know that, will they?"

"But what will happen when——" I began again, and again he had the answer before I'd finished the question.

"It'll go to the dead letter office, I expect," he told me. "And if he *is* dead, they'll dispose of him. If he's alive, I've no doubt they'll take good care of him. From the stamps I've gotten a notion living is easy and cheerful there, and the climate may do him good. His ancestors lived in a tropical country, you know."

That silenced my questions, and Harry picked up a stamp—the fifty-cent value—licked it, and placed it firmly on the box. Then he withdrew his hand and stepped back beside me.

Intently, we watched the parcel.

For a moment, nothing whatever happened.

And then, just as disappointment was gathering on Harry Norris's countenance, the box holding Thomas à Becket rose slowly into the air, turned like a compass needle, and began to drift with increasing speed toward the open window.

By the time it reached the window, it was moving with tremendous velocity. It shot through and into the open. We rushed to the window and saw it moving upward in a westerly direction, above the Manhattan skyline.

And then, as we stared, it began to be vague in outline, misty, and, an instant later, had vanished entirely. Because of its speed, I suggested, the same way a rifle bullet is invisible.

But Harry had another idea. He shook his head as we stepped back toward the center of the room. There was a gleam of wild amazement in his eyes.

"No," he began, "I don't think that's the answer. I have a notion——"

What his notion was I never did find out. Because just then he stopped speaking, with his mouth still open, and I saw him stiffen. He was looking past me, and I turned to see what affected him so. And I suspect that I stiffened too.

Outside the window was the package we had just seen vanish. It hung there for a moment, then moved slowly into the room, gave a little swoop, and settled lightly onto the table from which, not two minutes before, it had left.

Harry and I rushed over to it, and our eyes must have popped out a bit.

Because the package was all properly canceled and postmarked, just as the letter had been. With the addition that across the corner, in large purple letters, somebody had stamped, *Return to Sender. No Such Person at this Address.*

"Well!" Harry said at last. It wasn't exactly adequate, but it was all either of us could think of. Then, inside the box, Thomas à Becket let out a squawl.

I cut the cords and lifted the lid. Thomas à Becket leaped out with an animation he had not shown in years. He dropped to the floor and began to stalk back and forth, making a little spitting noise as if in indignation.

There was no denying it. Instead of killing him, his trip to El Dorado, brief as it was, had done him good. He looked five years younger.

Harry Norris was turning the box over in his hands, his expression perplexed.

"What I can't get over," he remarked, "is that there really *is* such an address as 711 Elysian Fields Avenue. I swear I just made it up on the spur of the moment."

"There's more to it than that," I reminded him. "The very fact that the package came back. We didn't put any return address on it."

"So we didn't," Harry agreed. "Yet they knew just where to return it to, didn't they? You know, these El Dorado people have a very remarkable postal system. There are some features of it Washington might copy with profit."

He pondered for a moment longer. Then he put the box down.

"I'm beginning to think," he said with an odd expression on his face, "that there is more to this than we realize. A great deal more. I suspect the whole truth is a lot more exciting than we have any notion of. As for this Federated States of El Dorado, I have a theory——"

But he didn't tell me what his theory was. Instead, that three-dollar chocolate-and-ivory stamp caught his eye again, and he broke off to pick it up.

"Jove," he whispered, more to himself than to me—he was given occasionally to these archaic ejaculations —"she's beautiful. Heavenly! With a model like that an artist could paint masterpieces. Even an artist like myself. To meet her I'd give—I'd give—— Well, almost anything."

"I'm afraid you'd have to go to El Dorado to do

that," I suggested flippantly, and Harry started.

"So I would! And I'm perfectly willing to do it, too. Listen! These stamps suggest this El Dorado place must be rather fascinating. What do you say we both pay it a visit? We neither of us have any ties to keep us, and——"

"Go there just so you can meet the girl who was the model for that stamp?" I demanded.

"Why not? Can you think of a better reason?" he asked me. "I can give you more. For one thing, the climate. Look how much better the cat is. His little excursion took years off his age. Must be a highly healthful place. Maybe it'll make a young man of you again. And besides——"

But he didn't have to go on. I was already convinced. As he said, those stamps conveyed the impression that the Federated States of El Dorado must be a place of surpassing interest.

"All right," I agreed. "We'll take the first boat. But when we get there, how will we——"

"By logic," Harry shot back. "Purely by logic. The girl must have posed for an artist, mustn't she? And the postmaster general of El Dorado must know who the artist is, mustn't he? We'll go straight to the postmaster general. He'll direct us to the artist. The artist will give us her name and address. Could anything be simpler?"

I hadn't realized how easy it would be. Now some of his impatience was getting into my own blood.

"Maybe we won't have to take a boat," I suggested. "Maybe there's a plane service. That would save——"

"Boat!" Harry Norris snorted, stalking back and forth across the room and waving his hands. "Plane! You can take boats and planes if you want to. I've got a better idea. I'm going to El Dorado by mail!"

Until I saw how beautifully simple his idea was, I was a bit stunned. But he quickly pointed out that Thomas à Becket had made the trip, and come back, without injury. If a cat could do it, a man could.

There wasn't a thing in the way except the choice of a destination. It would be rather wasted effort to go, only to be sent back ignominiously for want of proper addressing.

"I have that figured out too," Harry told me promptly when I voiced the matter. "The first person I'd go to see anyway when I got there would be the postmaster general. *He* must exist, certainly. And mail addressed to him would be the easiest of all to deliver. So why not kill two birds with one stone by posting myself to his office?"

That answered all my objections. It was as sound and sensible a plan as I'd ever heard.

"Why," Harry Norris added with rising excitement, "I may be having dinner with the girl tonight! Pomegranates beneath a gold-washed moon, with Pan piping in the shadows and nymphs dancing on the velvet green!"

Then he grinned, a little sheepish at having let his imagination run away so.

"At any rate," he said, "having dinner with her. Now to settle the details. We've got three stamps left—nine dollars' worth altogether. That should be enough.

I'm a bit lighter; you've been taking on weight lately, I see. Four dollars should carry me—the one and the three. That leaves the five-dollar for you. As for the address, we'll write that on tags and tie them to our wrists. You have tags, haven't you? Yes, here's a couple in this drawer. Now give me that pen and ink. Something like this ought to do very well . . ."

He wrote, then held the tags out to me. They were just alike. *Office of the Postmaster General,* they said. *Nirvana, Federated States of El Dorado. Perishable. Handle With Care.*

"Now," he said, "we'll each tie one to a wrist . . ."

But I drew back. Somehow I couldn't quite nerve myself to it. Delightful as were the prospects he had painted of the place, the idea of posting myself into the unknown, the way I had sent off Thomas à Becket, did something queer to me.

I told him I would join him. I would take the first boat, or plane, and meet him there, say at the principal hotel. But bring myself to go by mail I couldn't.

Harry was disappointed, but he was too impatient by now to argue.

"Well," he agreed, "all right. But if for any reason you can't get a boat or plane, you'll use that last stamp to join me?"

I promised faithfully that I would. With that he held out his right wrist and I tied a tag about it. Then he took up the one-dollar stamp, moistened it, and applied it to the tag. He had the three-dollar one in his hand when the doorbell rang.

"In a minute," he was saying, "or maybe in less, I

shall probably be in the fairest land man's imagination has ever been able to picture. And then——"

"Wait!" I called, and hurried out to answer the bell. I don't know whether he heard me or not. He was just lifting that second stamp to his tongue to moisten it when I turned away, and that was the last I ever saw of him.

When I came back, with the package in my hands—the doorbell had been rung by the messenger from the bookshop, delivering the atlas we had ordered—Harry Norris was gone.

Thomas à Becket was sitting up and staring toward the window. The curtains were still fluttering. I hurried over. But Norris was not in sight.

Well, I thought, he must have put on that stamp he had in his hand, not knowing I'd left the room. I could see him, in my mind's eye, that very moment being deposited on his feet in the office of an astonished postmaster general.

Then it occurred to me I might as well find out just where the Federated States of El Dorado were, after all. So I ripped the paper off the large volume the bookstore had sent and began to leaf through it.

When I had finished, I sat in silence for a while. From time to time I glanced at the unused tag and that uncanceled stamp still lying on my desk. Then I made my decision.

I got up and fetched Harry's bag. It was summer, luckily, and he had brought mostly light clothing. To it I added anything of mine I thought he might be able to use, including a carton of cigarettes, and pen and ink, on the chance he might want to write me.

As an afterthought I added a small Bible.

Then I strapped the bag shut and affixed the tag to it. I wrote *Harry Norris* above the address, pasted that last El Dorado stamp to it, and waited.

In a moment the bag rose in the air, floated to the window, out, and began to speed away.

It would reach there, I figured, before Harry had had time to leave the postmaster general's office, and I hoped he might send me a postcard or something by way of acknowledgment. But he didn't. Perhaps he couldn't.

. . . At this point Morks stopped, as if he had finished his story. But unnoticed, Malcolm had left our little group for a moment. Now he came pushing back into it with a large atlas in his hands.

"So that's what became of your set of rarities!" he said, with a scarcely veiled sneer. "Very interesting and entertaining. But there's one point I want to clear up. The stamps were issued by the Federated States of El Dorado, you say. Well, I've just been looking through this atlas, and there's no such place on earth."

Morks looked at him, his melancholy countenance calm.

"I know it," he said. "That's why, after glancing through my own atlas that day, I didn't keep my promise to Harry Norris and use that last stamp to join him. I'm sorry now. When I think of how Harry must be enjoying himself there——. But it's no good regretting what I did or didn't do. I couldn't help it. The truth is that my nerve failed me, just for a moment then, when I discovered there *was* no such place as the Federated States of El Dorado—on earth, I mean."

And sadly he shook his head.

"I've often wished I knew where my father got those stamps," he murmured, almost to himself; then fell into a meditative silence.

The Wonderful Day

I

DANNY WAS CROUCHED on the stairs, listening to the grownups talk in the living room below. He wasn't supposed to be there. He was supposed to be in bed, since he was still recovering from the chicken pox.

But it got lonely being in bed all the time, and he wasn't able to resist slipping out and down in his wool pajamas, to hear Dad and Mom, and Sis and Uncle Ben and Aunt Anna talking.

Dad—he was Dr. Norcross, and everybody went to him when they were sick—and the others were playing bridge. Sis, who was in high school, was studying her Latin, not so hard that she couldn't take part in the conversation.

They were mostly talking about other people in Locustville, which was such a small town everybody knew everybody else, well enough to talk about them, anyway.

"Locustville!" That was Mom, with a sigh. "I know it's a pretty town, with the river and the trees and the woods around it, and Tom has a good practice here. But the people! If only something would shake some of them out of themselves, and show them how petty and malicious and miserable they are!"

"Like Nettie Peters," Dad said, his tone dry. Danny knew Miss Peters. Always hurrying over to some neighbor to talk about somebody. Whisper-whisper-whisper. Saying nasty things. "She's the source of most of the gossip in this town. If ever there was a woman whose tongue was hinged in the middle and wagged at both ends, it's she."

Uncle Ben laughed.

"Things would be better here," he remarked, "if the money were better distributed. If Jacob Earl didn't own or have a mortgage on half the town, there might be more free thought and tolerance. But nobody in debt to him dares open his mouth."

"Funny thing," Dad put in, "how some men have a knack of making money at other men's expense. Everything Jacob Earl touches seems to mint money for him—money that comes out of someone else's pocket. Like the gravel land he got from John Wiggins. I'd like to see the process reversed sometime."

"But for real miserliness"—that was Aunt Anna, indignant—"Luke Hawks takes all the prizes. I've seen him come into the Fair-Square store to buy things for his children, and the trouble he had letting go of his money, you'd have thought it stuck to his fingers!"

"It's a question," Dad said, "which is worse, miserliness or shiftlessness. Miserliness, I suppose, because most shiftless people are at least good-hearted. Like Henry Jones. Henry wishes for more things and does less to get them than any man in Christendom. If wishes were horses, Henry would have the biggest herd this side of the Mississippi."

"Well, there are some nice people in Locustville," Sis broke into the conversation. "I don't care what that old gossip Miss Peters says, or that stuck-up Mrs. Norton either; I think Miss Avery, my English and gym teacher, is swell. She isn't very pretty, but she's nice.

"There are little silver bells in her voice when she talks, and if that Bill Morrow—whose dad owns the implement factory, and who takes time off to coach the football team—wasn't a dope, he'd have fallen for her long ago. She's crazy about him, but too proud to show it, and that silly Betty Norton has made him think he's wonderful by playing up to him all the time."

"If he marries Betty," Aunt Anna said, "the town won't be able to hold Mrs. Norton any more. She's already so puffed up with being the wife of the bank president and the leader of the town's social life, she'd just swell up a little more and float away like a balloon if she got the Morrow Implement Company for a son-in-law."

Everybody laughed, and the conversation slowly died away.

Mom mentioned how much she disliked the two-faced Minerva Benson who was so nice to people's faces and worked against them behind their backs.

Sis said that Mr. Wiggins, who ran the bookstore, was a nice little man who ought to marry Miss Wilson, the dressmaker, a plain little woman who would be as pretty as a picture if she *looked* the way she *was*.

But he never would, Sis said, because he hadn't any money and would be ashamed to ask a woman to marry him when he couldn't even earn his own living.

Then they went back to bridge. Danny was feeling sort of weak and shaky, so he hurried back to bed before Mom could catch him. He crawled in and pulled the blankets up over him, and then his hand reached under the pillow and pulled out the funny thing he'd found in the old chest where he kept his games and skates and things.

It had been wrapped in a soft piece of leather, and he had found it in a little space behind one of the drawers. There was a name inked on the leather, *Jonas Norcross*. Dad's grandfather had been named Jonas, so it might have been his originally.

The thing was a little pointed piece of ivory, sharp at the tip and round at the bottom, as if it had been sawed off the very end of an elephant's tusk. Only there was a fine spiral line in it, like a snail's shell, that made Danny think maybe it hadn't come from an elephant, but from an animal he had seen in a book once—an animal like a horse, with one long horn over its nose. He couldn't remember the name. It was all yellow with age, and on the bottom was carved a funny mark, all cross lines, very intricate. Maybe it was Chinese writing. Jonas Norcross had been captain of a clipper ship in the China trade, so it might have come all the way from China.

Lying in bed, Danny held the bit of ivory in his hand. It gave out a warmth to his fingers that was nice. Holding it tight, he thought of a picture in his book about King Arthur's Round Table—a picture of Queen Guinevere of the golden hair. Probably Sis had meant Miss Wilson ought to be as pretty as that picture.

Grownups' talk wasn't always easy to understand, the way they said things that weren't so.

Danny yawned. Wouldn't it be funny, though—— He yawned again, and the weight of drowsiness descending on him closed his eyes. But not before one last thought had floated through his mind.

As it came to him, a queer little breeze seemed to spring up in the room. It fluttered the curtains and rattled the window shade. For just a second Danny felt almost as if somebody was in the room with him. Then it was gone, and smiling at his amusing thought, Danny slept.

II

Henry Jones woke that morning with the smell of frying bacon in his nostrils. He yawned and stretched, comfortably. There was a clock on the bureau on the other side of the room, but it was too much trouble to look at it.

He looked at where the sunshine, coming in the window, touched the carpet. That told him it was just onto nine.

Downstairs pans were rattling. Martha was up and about, long ago. And just about ready to get impatient with him for lingering in bed.

"Ho *huuuum!*" Henry yawned, and pushed down the covers. "I wish I was up an' dressed aw-ready."

As if it were an echo to his yawn, a shrill whickering sound reached him from the direction of his large, untidy back yard. Disregarding it, Henry slid into his trousers and shirt, his socks and shoes, put on a tie, combed his hair casually, and ambled down to the dining room.

"Well!" his wife, Martha, commented tartly, appearing in the doorway with a platter in her hands as he slumped down into his chair. "It's after nine. If you're going to look for work today, you should have been started long ago!"

Henry shook his head dubiously as she set the bacon and eggs in front of him.

"I dunno if I ought to go tramping around today," he muttered. "Don't feel so well. Mmm, that looks good. But I kind of wish we could have sausage oncet in a while."

From the rear yard came another high whinny that went unnoticed.

"Sausage is expensive," Martha told him. "When you get an honest job, maybe we can afford some."

"There's Hawks," Henry remarked, with interest,

peering out the front window as a lean, long-faced man strode past the house, with a pleasant but shabbily-dressed little woman trotting meekly at his side. "Guess Millie has talked him into laying out some money for new things for the kids at last. It's only about once a year she gets him to loosen up."

"And then you'd think, to look at him, he was dying," his wife commented, "just because he's buying a couple of pairs of two-dollar shoes for two as nice youngsters as ever lived. He begrudges them every mouthful they eat, almost."

"Still," Henry said, wagging his head wisely, "I wish I had the money he has stacked away."

From the rear yard came a sound of galloping hooves. Martha was too intent on scolding Henry to notice it.

"Wish, wish, wish!" she stormed. "But never work, work, work! Oh, Henry, you're the most exasperating man alive!"

"Martha, I'm not worthy of you," Henry sighed. "I wish you had a better husband. I mean it."

This time the whinnying behind the house was a concerted squeal from many throats, too loud to go unnoticed. Henry's buxom wife started, looked puzzled, and hurried out to the kitchen. A moment later her screech reached Henry's ears.

"Henry! The back yard's full of horses! Plunging and kicking all over the place!"

The news was startling enough to overcome Henry's early-morning lethargy. He joined his wife at the kitchen window and stared with popping eyes at the big rear yard.

It was full—anyway, it seemed full—of animals. Martha had called them horses. They weren't exactly horses. But they weren't ponies either. They were too small to be the one and too big to be the other. And they were covered with longish hair, had wild flowing manes, and looked strong and savage enough to lick their weight in tigers.

"Well, I'll be deuced!" Henry exclaimed, his round countenance vastly perplexed. "I wish I knew where those critters came from."

"Henry!" Martha wailed, clutching his arm. "Now there are five!"

There had been four of them, trotting about the yard, nosing at the wreck of the car Henry had once driven, thumping with their hooves the board fence that penned them in. But now there were, indeed, five.

"G-gosh!" Henry gulped, his Adam's apple working up and down. "We must have counted wrong. Now, how do you suppose they got in there?"

"But what kind of horses are they, Henry?" Martha asked, holding to his arm still, as if for protection, in a way she hadn't for years. "And whom do you suppose they belong to?"

Henry put an arm around Martha's plump waist and applied a reassuring pressure.

"I wish I knew, Martha," he muttered. "I wish I knew."

"Henry!" There was real fright in his wife's voice. "Now there are six!"

"Seven," Henry corrected weakly. "The other two

just—just sort of appeared."

Together they gazed at the seven shaggy ponies which were trotting restlessly about the yard, nosing at the fence as if seeking escape from the limited space.

No more appeared; and seeing the number remain stable, Henry and Martha gained more self-possession.

"Henry," his wife said with severity, as if somehow blaming him, "there's something queer happening. Nobody ever saw horses like those in Indiana before."

"Maybe they belong to a circus," Henry suggested, staring in fascination at the seven uncouth beasts.

"Maybe they belong to us!"

"Us?" Henry's jaw dropped. "How could they belong to us?"

"Henry," his wife told him, "you've got to go out and see if they're branded. I remember reading anybody can claim a wild horse if it hasn't been branded. And those are wild horses if I ever saw any."

Of course, Martha never *had* seen any wild horses, but her words sounded logical. Her husband, however, made no motion toward the back door.

"Listen, Martha," he said, "you stay here and watch. Don't let anybody into the yard. I'm going to get Jake Harrison, at the stable. He used to be a horse trader. He'll know what those things are and if they belong to us, if anybody does."

"All right, Henry," his wife agreed—the first time he could remember her agreeing with him in two years —"but hurry. Please do hurry."

"I will!" Henry vowed; and without even snatching

up his hat, he shot away.

Jake Harrison, the livery stable owner, came back with him unwillingly, half dragged in Henry's excitement. But when he stood in the kitchen and stared out at the yard full of horses, his incredulity vanished.

"Good Lord!" he gasped. "Henry, where'd you get 'em?"

"Never mind that," Henry told him. "Just tell me what *are* they?"

"Mongolian ponies," the lanky horse dealer informed him. "The exact kind of ponies old Ghengis Khan's men rode on when they conquered most of the known world. I've seen pictures of them in books. Imagine it! Mongolian ponies here in Locustville!"

"Well," Martha asked, with withering scorn, "aren't you going out to see if they're branded? Or are you two men afraid of a lot of little ponies?"

"I guess they won't hurt us," the stable owner decided, "if we're careful. Come on, Henry, let's see if I'm still any good at lassoing. Mis' Jones, can I use this hank of clothesline?"

Henry opened the kitchen door and followed Jake Harrison out into the yard. At their arrival the seven ponies—he was glad to see the number hadn't changed in his absence—stopped their restless trotting and lifted their heads to stare at the men.

Jake made a noose out of the clothesline and began to circle it above his head. The ponies snorted and reared, suspiciously. Picking the smallest one, the tall man let the noose go, and it settled over the creature's thick neck.

The pony's nostrils flared. It reared and beat the air with its unshod front hooves as the other six ponies broke and scampered to the opposite end of the yard.

Jake Harrison drew the loop tight and approached the pony, making soothing sounds. It quieted and, as the two men came close, let Jake put his hands on it.

"Yes, sir," the stable owner exclaimed, "a real honest-to-Homer Mongolian pony. The long hair is to keep the cold out, up in the mountains of Tibet. Now let's see if there's any brand. None on its hide. Let's see its hoof."

The pony let him lift its left forefoot without protest, and Henry, bending close, let out a whoop.

"Look, Jake!" he yelled. "It's branded! With my name! These critters are mine!"

Together they stared. Cut into the hard horn, in neat letters, was the name HENRY JONES.

Jake straightened.

"Yours, all right," he agreed. "Now, Henry, stop making a mystery and tell me where these animals came from."

Henry's jubilance faded. He shook his head.

"Honest, Jake, I don't know. I wish I did. . . . *Look out!*"

The tall man leaped back. Between them an eighth pony had appeared, so close that its flanks brushed against them.

"W-where——" Jake stuttered, backing away toward the door in the fence and fumbling for the catch. "Where——"

"That's what I don't know!" Henry joined him.

"That's what I wish—— No, I don't either! I don't wish anything at all!"

The phantom pony that had appeared directly before them, wispy and tenuous as darkish smoke, promptly vanished.

Henry mopped his face.

"Did you see what I saw?" he asked; and Jake, swallowing hard, nodded.

"You st-started to wish for something, and it st-started to appear," he gobbled, and thrust open the door in the board fence. "Let's get out o' here."

"When I started to wish—— Oh, jiminy crickets!" Henry groaned. "That's how the others happened. When I wished. Do you suppose—— Do you——"

Pale-faced, they stared at each other. Slowly the stableman nodded.

"Lord!" the ashen Henry whispered. "I never believed such a thing could happen. I wish now I'd never——"

This time the words weren't fully out of his mouth before the ninth pony struck the earth with a sudden plop directly before them.

It was too much. Henry broke and ran, and Jake followed at his heels. The pony, interestedly, chased them. Its brothers, not to be left behind, streamed through the opening in the fence, whickering gleefully.

When Henry and Jake brought up, around the corner of the house, they were just in time to look back and see the last of the beasts trotting out into Main Street. Nine wicked whinnies cut through the morning quiet. Nine sets of small hooves pounded.

"They're stampeding!" Henry shrilled. "Jake, we got to round 'em up before they do lots of damage. Oh, Jehosephat, I wish this hadn't ever happened!"

Neighing raucously, the tenth pony kicked up its heels, throwing dirt in their faces, and set off at a gallop after the others.

III

About the time Henry Jones was running for Jake Harrison, Luke Hawks was fingering a boy's woolen suit with lean, predatory digits.

"This be the cheapest?" he asked, and being assured that it was—all the clerks in Locustville knew better than to show him anything but the least expensive— he nodded.

"I'll take it," he said, and grudgingly reached for his hip pocket.

"Don't you think the material is kind of thin, Luke?" little Emily Hawks asked, a note of pleading in her voice. "Last winter Billy had colds all the time, and Ned——"

The man did not bother to answer. With the well-filled wallet in his left hand, he inserted thumb and forefinger and brought out a twenty-dollar bill.

"Here," he said. "And I've got eight dollars forty cents coming."

Taking the bill and starting to turn away, the clerk turned abruptly back. Luke Hawks had snatched the money from his hand.

"Is anything——" he began, and stopped. Testily

the man was still holding out the note.

"Take it," he snapped. "Don't make me stand here waiting."

"Yes, sir." The clerk apologized, and took a firmer hold. But he could not take the bill from Luke Hawks. He pulled. Hawks's hand jerked forward. Scowling, the lean man drew his hand back. The money came with it.

"What's the matter, Luke?" Emily Hawks muttered. Her husband favored her with a frown.

"Some glue on it, or something," he muttered. "It stuck to my fingers. I'll get another bill out, young man."

He put the twenty back into the wallet—where it went easily enough—and drew out two tens. But these would not leave his hand, either.

Luke Hawks was beginning to go a little pale. He transferred the notes to his left hand. But though his left hand could take them from his right, the clerk could take them from neither. Whenever he tugged at it, the money simply would not come loose. It stuck as close to Luke Hawks's fingers as if it were part of his skin.

A red flush crept into the man's cheeks. He could not meet his wife's gaze.

"I—I dunno——" he muttered. "I'll lay it down. You pick it up."

Carefully he laid a ten-dollar bill on the counter, spread his fingers wide, and lifted his hand. To his horror and fright, the bit of green paper came with it, adhering firmly to his fingertips.

"Luke Hawks," his wife said sturdily, "it's a judgment on you. The good Lord has put a curse on your money."

"Hush!" Hawks warned. "Netty Peters has come in the store and is looking. She'll hear you and go gabbing nonsense——"

"It is not nonsense!" his wife stated. "It's the truth. Your money will not leave your fingers."

Luke Hawks went deathly pale again. With a strangled curse, he snatched out all the money in his wallet and tried to throw it down on the counter. To his intense relief, one folded green slip fluttered down, though the rest remained in his hand.

"There!" he gasped. "It ain't so! Boy, how much is that?"

The clerk reached for the paper.

"It—it's a cigar coupon, sir," he reported, his face wooden.

Luke Hawks wilted then. He thrust all his money into the ancient pigskin wallet and, being careful that his fingers touched only the leather, held it out to his wife.

"Here!" he directed. "You pay him, Emily."

Emily Hawks folded her arms and looked straight into his frightened eyes.

"Luke Hawks," she said, in a firm, clear voice that carried through the entire store, "for eight years my life has been made a misery by your mean, grasping ways. Now you can't spend any of your money. You'll starve to death before you can even spend a nickel for bread.

"And I've a good mind to let you. If I don't buy anything for you, you can be sure no one will give it to you. The people of this town would laugh themselves sick seeing you with your hands full of money, begging for a bite to eat. They wouldn't give it to you, either."

Luke Hawks knew they wouldn't. He stared down at his wife who had never before dared act like this.

"No," he protested. "Emily, don't say that. Here, you take the money. Spend it as you want. Get the things we need. I'll leave it all to you. You—you can even get the next most expensive clothes for the boys."

"You mean you want me to handle the money from now on?" Emily Hawks demanded, and her husband nodded.

"Yes, Emily," he gasped. "Take it. Please take it."

His wife took the wallet—which left Luke Hawks's hands readily enough—and counted the money in it.

"Five hundred dollars," she said aloud, thoughtfully. "Luke, hadn't you better give me a check for what you've got in the bank? If I'm to do all the buying, the money'll have to be in my hands."

"A check!" Luke exclaimed. "That's it! I don't need money! I'll pay by check."

"Try it," Emily invited. "That's the same as cash, isn't it?"

Luke tried it. The check would not leave his fingers either. It only tore to pieces when the clerk tugged at it.

After that, he capitulated. He took out his book

and signed a blank check, which Emily was able to take. She then filled it in for herself for the entire balance in the bank—twenty thousand dollars, Luke Hawks admitted with strangled reluctance.

After that she tucked the check into the bosom of her dress.

"Now, Luke," she suggested, "you might as well go on home. I'll go to the bank and deposit this to my account. Then I'll do the rest of the shopping. I won't need you."

"But how'll you get the things home?" her husband asked weakly.

Emily Hawks was already almost to the door—out which Netty Peters had just dashed to spread the news through the town. But she paused long enough to turn and smile brightly at her pale and perspiring husband.

"I'll have the man at the garage drive me out with them," she answered. "In the car I'm going to buy after I leave the bank, Luke."

IV

Miss Wilson looked up from her sewing at the sound of galloping hooves in the street outside her tiny shop.

She was just in time to see a small swift figure race by. Then, before she could wonder what it was, she caught sight of herself in the big mirror customers used when trying on the dresses she made.

Her whole name was Alice Wilson. But it was years since anyone had called her by her first name. She was thirty-three, as small and plain as a church mouse——

But she wasn't! Miss Wilson stared open-mouthed at her reflection. She wasn't mouselike any longer. She was—yes, really—almost pretty!

A length of dress goods forgotten in one hand, a needle suspended in midair in the other, Alice Wilson stared at the woman in the glass. She saw a small woman, with a smiling, pink-and-white face, over which a stray lock of golden hair had fallen from the piled-up mass of curls on top of her head—curls that gave out a soft and shining light.

The woman in the mirror had soft, warm red lips and blue eyes of sky-azure clearness and depth. Alice Wilson stared, and smiled in sheer delight. The image smiled back.

Wonderingly, Alice touched her face with her fingers. What had happened? What kind of a trick were her eyes playing on her? How——

The clatter of hurrying footsteps made her jump. Netty Peters, her sharp face alight with excitement, her head thrust forward on her skinny neck like a running chicken's, ran in. Miss Wilson's dressmaking shop, the closest place to the Fair-Square store, was her first stop on her tour to spread the news of Luke Hawks's curse.

"Miss Wilson," she gobbled breathlessly, "what do you think——"

"*She thinks you've come to spread some scandal or other, that's what she thinks,*" a shrill, file-like voice interrupted.

The voice seemed to come from her own mouth. Netty Peters glared.

"Miss Wilson," she snapped, "if you think ventriloquism is funny when I'm trying to tell you—*just like you're going to tell everybody else!*" the second voice broke in, and Netty Peters felt faint. The words *had* come from her own mouth!

She put her hands to her throat; and because her mind was blank with fright, her tongue went busily ahead with what she had planned to say.

"I saw Luke Hawks—*just as you see everything*"— that was the shrill, second voice, alternating with her normal one—"in the Fair-Square store and he and his wife—*were minding their own business, something you might do*—were buying clothes for their poor starved children whom they treat so shamefully—*trust you to get that in!*—when Mr. Hawks tried to pay the clerk— *and you were watching to see how much they spent.* The money wouldn't leave his fingers. *Did you ever think how many people would be happy if sometimes the words wouldn't leave your throat?*"

The town gossip ceased. Her words had become all jumbled together, making no sense, like two voices trying to shout each other down. There was a strange fluttering in her throat. As if she were talking with two tongues at the same time. . . .

Miss Wilson was staring at her strangely, and Netty Peters saw for the first time the odd radiance in Miss Wilson's hair, the new sweetness in her features.

Incoherent words gurgled in the older woman's throat. Terror glazed her eyes. She turned and, with a queer sobbing wail, fled.

Alice Wilson was still looking after her in bewilderment when another figure momentarily darkened the doorway. It was Mr. Wiggins, who owned the unprofitable bookstore on the other side of her dressmaking establishment.

Ordinarily Mr. Wiggins was a shy, pale-faced man, his thirty-eight years showing in the stoop of his shoulders, his eyes squinting behind thick glasses. He often smiled, but it was the small, hopeful smile of a man who didn't dare not to smile for fear he might lose heart altogether.

But today, this day of strange happenings, Mr. Wiggins was standing erect. His hair was rumpled, his glasses were awry, and his eyes blazed with excitement.

"Miss Wilson!" he cried. "The most amazing thing has happened! I had to tell somebody. I hope you don't mind my bursting in to tell you."

Alice Wilson stared at him, and instantly forgot about the strange thing that had happened to her.

"Oh, no!" she answered. "Of course I don't. I—I'm glad!"

Outside there were more sounds of galloping hooves, shrill squeals, and men's voices shouting.

"There seems to be a herd of wild ponies loose in the town," Mr. Wiggins told Miss Wilson. "One almost knocked me down, racing along the sidewalk as I was coming here. Miss Wilson, you'll never believe it, what I was going to tell you. You'll have to see for yourself. Then you won't think I'm mad."

"Oh, I'd never think that!" Miss Wilson assured him.

Scarcely hearing her, Mr. Wiggins seized her by the hand and almost dragged her to the door. A flush of warm pleasure rose into Miss Wilson's cheeks at the touch of his hand.

A little breathless, she ran beside him, out the shop door, down a dozen yards, and into the gloom of his tiny, unpatronized bookstore.

On the way, she barely had a glimpse of three or four shaggy ponies snorting and wheeling farther up the street, with Henry Jones and Jake Harrison, assisted by a crowd of laughing men and boys, trying to catch them.

Then Mr. Wiggins, trembling with excitement, was pushing her down into an old overstuffed chair.

"Miss Wilson," he said tensely, "I was sitting right here when in came Jacob Earl, not fifteen minutes ago. You know how he walks—big and pompous, as if he owned the earth. I knew what he wanted. He wanted the thousand dollars I owe him, that I borrowed to buy my stock of books with. And I didn't have it. None of it.

"You remember when my aunt died last year, she left me that property down by the river that I sold to Jacob Earl for five hundred dollars? He pretended he was doing me a favor buying it, to help me get started in business.

"But then high-grade gravel was discovered on the land, and now it's worth at least fifteen thousand dollars. I learned Earl knew about the gravel all the time. But in spite of that, he wanted the thousand he loaned me."

"Yes, oh yes!" Miss Wilson exclaimed. "He would. But what did you *do*, Mr. Wiggins?"

Mr. Wiggins combed back his disheveled hair with his fingers.

"I told him I didn't have it. And he took off his glove—his right glove—and told me if I didn't have it by tomorrow, he'd have to attach all my books and fixtures. And then he put his hand down on top of my antique brass Chinese luck piece. And guess what happened!"

"Oh, I couldn't!" Miss Wilson whispered. "I never could!"

"Look!" Mr. Wiggins's voice trembled. He snatched up a large dust cloth that hid something on the counter just in front of Miss Wilson's eyes. Underneath the cloth was a squat little Chinese god, about a foot high, sitting with knees crossed and holding a bowl in his lap. On his brass countenance was a sly smile, and his mouth was open in a round O of great amusement.

As Miss Wilson stared at him, a small gold coin popped out of the little god's mouth and landed with a musical chink in the bowl in his lap!

Alice Wilson gasped. "Oh, John!" she cried, using Mr. Wiggins's Christian name for the first time in her life. "Is it—is it money?"

"Chinese money," Mr. Wiggins told her. "And the bowl is full of it. A gold coin comes out of his mouth every second. The first one came out right after Mr. Earl put his hand on the god's head. Look!"

He scooped up the contents of the bowl and held them out, let the gold coins rain into Miss Wilson's lap.

Incredulously she picked one up.

It was a coin as large perhaps as an American nickel. In the center was punched a square hole. All around the edges were queer Oriental ideographs. And the piece of money was as fresh and new and shiny as if it had just come from the mint.

"Is it real gold?" Miss Wilson asked tremulously.

"Twenty carats pure at least!" John Wiggins assured her. "Even if it is Chinese money, the coins must be worth five dollars apiece just for the metal. And look—the bowl is half full again."

They stared wide-eyed and breathless at the little grinning god. Every second, as regularly as clockwork, another gold coin popped out of his open mouth.

"It's as if—as if he were coining them!" John Wiggins whispered.

"Oh, it's wonderful!" Alice Wilson told him, with rapture. "John, I'm so glad! For your sake. Now you can pay off Earl."

"In his own coin!" the man chortled. "Because he started it happening, you know, so you could call it his own coin. Perhaps he pressed a secret spring or something that released the coins from where they were hidden inside the god. I don't know.

"But the funny thing is, he couldn't pick them up! He tried to pretend he had just dropped the first couple, but they rolled out of the bowl and right across the floor when he reached for them. And then he began to get frightened. He grabbed up his hat and his gloves and ran out."

Then John Wiggins paused. He was looking down at

Alice Wilson, and for the first time he really saw the change that had occurred in her.

"Why," he said, "do you know, your hair is the same color as the coins?"

"Oh, it isn't!" Miss Wilson protested, blushing scarlet at the first compliment a man had paid her in ten years.

"It is," he insisted. "And you—you're lovely, Alice. I never realized before how lovely. You're as pretty as —as pretty as a picture!"

He looked down into her eyes and, without taking his gaze away, reached down and took her hands in his. He drew her up out of the chair and, still crimsoning with pleasure, Alice Wilson stood and faced him.

"Alice," John Wiggins said, "I've known you for a long time, and I've been blind. I guess worry blinded me. Or I'd have seen long ago how beautiful you are and would have known what I've just realized. I know I'm not much of a success as a man, but—— Alice, would you be my wife?"

Alice Wilson gave a little sigh and rested her face against his shoulder so that he might not see the tears in her eyes. Happiness had mostly eluded her until now, but this moment more than made up for all the years that were past.

John Wiggins put his arms about her, and behind them the little god grinned and went busily on with his minting. . . .

Jacob Earl stomped into the library in his home and locked the door behind him, with fingers that shook a little.

Throwing his hat, stick, and gloves down onto a chair, he groped for a cigar in his desk and lit it, by sheer force of will striving to quell the inward agitation that was shaking him.

Well, any man might feel shaken if he had put his hand down on a cold brass paperweight and had felt the thing twist in his grip as if alive, had felt a shock in his fingers like a sudden discharge of electricity, and then had seen the thing start to spout gold money. Real money!

Money—and Jacob Earl gazed down at his soft, plump white hands almost with fright—which had *life* in it. Because when he had tried to pick it up, it had eluded him. It had *dodged.*

Angrily he flung away his barely smoked cigar. Hallucinations! He'd been having a dizzy spell, or something. Maybe Wiggins had fixed up a trick to play on him. That was it, a trick!

The nerve of the man, giving him such a start! When he had finished with the little rabbit, he——

Jacob Earl did not quite formulate what he would do. But the mere thought of threatening somebody made him feel better. He'd decide later what retaliation he would make.

Right now, he'd get to work. He'd inventory his strong box. Nothing like handling hard, tangible possessions, like stocks and bonds and gold, to restore a man's nerves when he felt shaky.

He spun the combination of his safe, swung open

the heavy outer door, unlocked the inner door, and slid out first a weighty steel cash box locked by a massive padlock.

Weighty, because it held the one thing a man couldn't have too much of—gold. Pure gold ingots; worth five hundred dollars each. Fifteen thousand dollars' worth of them.

He'd had them since long before the government called in gold. And he was going to keep them, government or no. If he ever had to sell them, he'd claim they'd been forgotten, and found again by accident.

Jacob Earl flung open the lid of his gold cache. And his overly ruddy face turned a sudden pallid gray. Two of the ingots in the top layer were missing!

But no one could get into his safe. No one but himself. It wasn't possible that a thief——

Then the gray of his face turned to ashen white. He stared, his breath caught in his throat. As he stared, a third ingot had vanished. Evaporated. Into thin air. As if an unseen hand had closed over it and snatched it away.

But it wasn't possible! Such a thing couldn't happen.

And then the fourth ingot vanished. Transfixed by rage and fright, he put his hands down on the remaining yellow bars and pressed with all his might.

But presently the fifth of his precious chunks of metal slipped away from beneath his very fingers into nothingness. One instant it was there, and he could feel it. Then it was gone!

With a hoarse cry, Jacob Earl dropped the cash box.

He stumbled across the room to his telephone, got a number.

"Doctor?" he gasped. "Doctor Norcross? This is Jacob Earl. I—I——"

Then he bethought himself. This couldn't happen. This was madness. If he told anyone——

"Never mind, doctor!" he blurted. "Sorry to have troubled you. It's all right."

He hung up. And he sat there, all the rest of the day, sweat beading his brow, watching the shiny yellow oblongs that had fallen on the floor vanish one by one.

In another part of town, another hand crept toward the telephone—and drew back. Minerva Benson's hand. Minerva Benson had discovered her deformity almost the instant she had arisen, late that morning. The mirror had shown her the stiff, lifeless face affixed to her head. Thin, vicious, twisted, she had the features of a harpy.

With trembling fingers she touched her face again, in a wild hope that its ugliness might have vanished. Then she huddled closer on the end of the sofa in the darkened room, whose door was locked, blinds drawn.

She couldn't telephone. Because no one must see her like this. No one. Not even a doctor. . . .

And in her tiny spinsterish home Netty Peters also crouched, and also feared to telephone.

Feared, lest that strange, dreadful second voice begin to clack and rattle in her throat when she tried to talk, tried to ask Doctor Norcross to come.

Crouched, and felt her throat with fingers like frantic claws. And she was sure she could detect something moving in her throat like a thing alive.

V

Mrs. Edward Norton moved along the tree-shaded streets toward the downtown section of Locustville with all the self-conscious pride of a frigate entering a harbor under full sail.

She was a full-bodied woman—well built, she phrased it—and expensively dressed. Certainly she was the best-dressed woman in town, as befitted her position as leader of Locustville's social life and the most influential woman in town.

And today she was going to use her influence. She was going to have Janice Avery discharged as a teacher in the high school.

Distinctly she had seen the young woman *smoking* in her room, the previous evening, when she happened to be driving by. A woman who should be an example to the children she taught——

Mrs. Norton sailed along, indignation high in her. She had called first at Minerva Benson's home. Minerva was a member of the school board. But Minerva had said she was sick, and refused to see her.

Then she had tried Jacob Earl, the second member of the board. And he had been ill, too.

It was odd.

Now she was going directly to the office of Doctor Norcross. He was head of the school board. Not the kind of man she approved of for the 'position, of course——

Mrs. Norton paused. For the past few moments she had been experiencing a strange sensation of puffiness, of lightness. Was she ill too? Could she be feeling light-headed or dizzy?

But no, she was perfectly normal. Just a moment's upset, perhaps, from walking too fast.

She continued onward. What had she been thinking about? Oh, yes, Doctor Norcross. An able physician, perhaps, but his wife was really quite—well, quite a dowdy. . . .

Mrs. Norton paused again. A gentle breeze was blowing down the street and she—she was being swayed from side to side by it. Actually, it was almost pushing her off balance!

She took hold of a convenient lamppost. That stopped her from swaying. But——

She stared transfixed at her fingers. They were swollen and puffy. Her rings were cutting into them painfully. Could she have some awful——

Then she became aware of a strained, uncomfortable feeling all over her person. A feeling of being confined, intolerably pent-up in her clothing.

With her free hand she began to tug at herself, at first with puzzlement, then with terror. Her clothing was as tight on her as the skin of a sausage. It had shrunk! It was cutting off her circulation!

No, it hadn't. That wasn't true. She was growing! Puffing up! Filling out her clothes like a slowly expanding balloon.

Her corset was confining her diaphragm, making it impossible to breathe. She couldn't get air into her lungs.

She had some awful disease. That was what came of living in a dreadful, dirty place like Locustville, among backward, ignorant people who carried germs and——

At that instant the laces of Mrs. Norton's corset gave way. She could actually feel herself swell, bloat, puff out. Her arms were queer and hard to handle. The seams of her dress were giving away.

The playful breeze pushed her, and she swayed back and forth.

Her fingers slipped from the lamppost.

And she began to rise slowly, ponderously, into the air, like a runaway balloon.

Mrs. Edward Norton screamed. Piercingly. But her voice seemed lost, a thin wail that carried hardly twenty yards. This was unthinkable. This was impossible!

But it was happening.

Now she was a dozen feet above the sidewalk. Now twenty. And at that level she paused, spinning slowly around and around, her arms flopping like a frightened chicken's wings, her mouth opening and closing like a feeding goldfish's, but no sounds coming forth.

If anyone should see her now! Oh, if anyone should see her!

But no one did. The street was quite deserted. The houses were few, and set well back from the street. And the excitement downtown, the herd of strange ponies that all day had been kicking up their heels, as Henry Jones and his volunteer assistants tried to pen them up, had drawn every unoccupied soul in Locustville.

Mrs. Norton, pushed along by the gentle breeze, began to drift slowly northward toward the town limits.

Tree branches scraped her and ripped her stockings as she clutched unavailingly at them. A crow, attracted by the strange spectacle, circled around her several times, emitted a raucous squawk that might have been amusement, and flew off.

A stray dog, scratching fleas in the sunshine, saw her pass overhead and followed along underneath for a moment, barking furiously.

Mrs. Norton crimsoned with shame and mortification. Oh, if anyone saw her!

But if no one saw her, no one could help her. She did not know whether to pray for someone to come along or not. She was unhurt. Perhaps nothing worse was going to happen.

But to be sailing placidly through the air, twenty feet above the street, puffed up like a balloon!

The breeze had brought her out to a district marked for subdivision, but still vacant. Fruit trees grew upon the land. The playful wind, shifting its quarter, altered her course. In a moment she was drifting past the upper branches of gnarled old apple trees, quite hidden from the street.

Her clothes were torn, her legs and arms scratched, her hair was straggling down her back. And her indignation and fear of being seen began to give way to a sensation of awful helplessness. She, the most important woman in Locustville, to be blowing around among a lot of old fruit trees for crows to caw at and dogs to bark at and——

Mrs. Norton gasped. She had just risen another three feet.

With that she began to weep.

The tears streamed down her face. All at once she felt humble and helpless and without a thought for her dignity or her position. She just wanted to get down.

She just wanted to go home and have Edward pat her shoulder and say, "There, there," as he used to—a long time ago—while she had a good cry on his shoulder.

She was a bad woman, and she was being punished for it. She had been puffed up with pride, and this was what came of it. In the future, if ever she got down safely, she'd know better.

As if influenced by the remorseful thoughts, she began to descend slowly. Before she was aware of it, she had settled into the upper branches of a cherry tree, scaring away a flock of indignant birds.

And there she caught.

She had a lot of time in which to reflect before she saw Janice Avery swinging past along a short cut from the school to her home, and called to her.

Janice Avery got her down, with the aid of Bill

Morrow—who was the first person she could find when she ran back to the school to get aid.

Bill was just getting into his car to drive out to the football field, where he was putting the school team through spring practice, when she ran up; and at first he did not seem to understand what she was saying.

As a matter of fact, he didn't. He was just hearing her voice—a voice that was cool and sweet and lovely, like music against a background of distant silver bells.

Then, when he got it, he sprang into action.

"Good grief!" he exclaimed. "Mrs. Norton stuck up a tree picking cherries? I can't believe it."

But he got a ladder from the school and brought it, gulping at the sight of the stout, tearful woman caught in the crotch of the cherry tree.

A few moments later they had her down. Mrs. Norton made no effort to explain beyond the simple statement she had first made to Janice.

"I was picking cherries and I just got stuck!"

Wild as it was, it was better than the truth.

Bill Morrow brought his car as close as he could and Janice hurried her out to it, torn, scratched, bedraggled, red-eyed. They got her in without anyone else's seeing and drove her home.

Mrs. Norton sobbed out a choked thanks and fled into the house, to weep on the shoulders of her surprised husband.

Bill Morrow mopped his forehead and looked at Janice Avery. She wasn't pretty, but there was something lovely in her smile. And in her voice. A man could hear a voice like that all his life and not grow tired of it.

"Golly!" he exclaimed, as he slid behind the wheel of his car. "And Betty Norton is going to look just like that some day. Whew! Do you know, I'm a fool. I actually once thought of—— But never mind. Where can I take you?"

He grinned at her, and Janice Avery smiled back, little happy lines springing into life around the corners of her lips and her eyes.

"Well," she began, as the wide-shouldered young man kicked the motor into life, "you have to get to practice——"

"Practice is out!" Bill Morrow told her with great firmness as he let in the clutch. "We're going some place and talk!"

She sat back, content.

VI

The sun was setting redly as Dr. Norcross closed his office and swung off homeward with a lithe step.

It had been a strange day. Very strange. Wild ponies had been running through the town since morning, madly chased by the usually somnolent Henry Jones. From his window he had seen into the bookstore across the street and distinctively perceived John Wiggins and Alice Wilson embracing.

Then there had been that abortive phone call from an obviously agitated Jacob Earl. And he had positively seen Mrs. Luke Hawks going past in a brand-new car, with a young man at the wheel who seemed to be teaching her to drive. Whew!

There would be a lot to tell his wife tonight.

His reflections were cut short as he strode past Henry Jones's back yard, which lay on his homeward short-cut route.

A crowd of townsfolk were gathered about the door in the fence around the yard, and Dr. Norcross could observe others in the house, peering out the windows. Henry and Jake Harrison, mopping their faces with fatigue, stood outside peering into the yard through the cautiously opened doorway. And over the fence itself, he was able to see the tossing heads of many ponies, while their squeals cut the evening air.

"Well, Henry,"—that was Martha, who came around the corner of the house and pushed through the crowd about her husband—"you've rounded up all the horses all right. But how're you going to pay for the damage they did today? Now you'll have to go to work, in spite of yourself. Even if they aren't good for anything else they've accomplished *that!*"

There was an excitement on Henry's face Dr. Norcross had never seen there before.

"Sure, Martha, sure," he agreed. "I know I'll have to pay off the damage. But Jake and me, we've got plans for these hooved jackrabbits. Know what we're going to do?"

He turned, so all of the gathered crowd could hear his announcement.

"Jake and me, we're going to use that land of Jake's south of town to breed polo ponies!" he declared. "Yes, sir, we're going to cross these streaks of lightning with real polo ponies. We're gonna get a new breed with the speed of a whippet, the endurance of a mule, and the intelligence of a human.

"Anybody who saw these creatures skedaddle around town today knows that when we get a polo pony with their blood in it developed, it'll be something! Yes, sir, something! I wish——

"No, I don't! I don't wish for anything! Not a single solitary thing! I'm not gonna wish for anything ever again, either!"

Norcross grinned. Maybe Henry had something there. Then, noting that the sun had just vanished, he went home.

Up in his room, Danny Norcross woke groggily from a slumber that had been full of dreams. Half asleep still, he groped for and found the little piece of ivory he had kept beside him ever since he had fallen asleep the night before.

His brow wrinkled. He had been on the stair, listening to the grownups talk. They had said a lot of queer things. About horses, and money, and pictures. Then he had gotten back in bed and played with his bit of ivory for a while. Then he had had a funny thought, and sort of a wish——

The wish that had passed through his mind, as he had been falling asleep, had been that all the things Dad and Mom and the others had said would come true, because it would be so funny if they did.

So he had wished that just for one day, maybe, all

Henry Jones's wishes would be horses, and money would stick to Luke Hawks's fingers, and Jacob Earl would touch something that would coin money for somebody else for a change.

And, too, that Netty Peters's tongue really would be hinged in the middle and wag at both ends, and Mrs. Benson have two faces, and Mrs. Norton swell up and blow around like a balloon.

And that Miss Wilson would really be as pretty as a picture, and you could truly hear silver bells when Miss Avery talked.

That had been his wish.

But now, wide-awake and staring out the window at a sky all red because the sun had set, he couldn't quite remember it, try as he would. . . .

Crouched in her darkened room, Minerva Benson felt her head for the hundredth time. First with shuddering horror, then with hope, then with incredulous relief. The dreadful face was gone now.

But she would remember it, and be haunted by it forever in her dreams.

Netty Peters stared at herself in her mirror, her eyes wide and frightened. Slowly she took her hands from her throat. The queer fluttering was gone. She could talk again without that terrible voice interrupting.

But always after, when she began to speak, she would stop abruptly for fear it might sound again, in the middle of a sentence.

"I've decided, Luke," Mrs. Luke Hawks said with decision, "that we'll have the house painted and put in a new furnace. Then I'm going to take the children off on a little vacation.

"No, don't say anything! Remember, the money is in my name now, and I can spend it all, if I've a mind to. I can take it and go away to California, or any place. And no matter what you say or do, I'm not going to give it back!"

Jacob Earl uttered a groan. The last gold ingot had just vanished from the floor of his library.

John Wiggins turned. The tiny *chink-chink* that had sounded all afternoon had ceased. The little god still grinned, but the coins were no longer coming from his mouth.

"He's quit," the little man announced to the flushed and radiant Alice Wilson. "But we don't care. Look how much money came out of him. Why, there must be fifteen thousand dollars there!

"Alice, we'll take a trip around the world. And we'll take him back to China, where he came from. He deserves a reward."

With the red afterglow tinting the little lake beside which he had parked the car, Bill Morrow turned. His arm was already about Janice Avery's shoulders.

So it really wasn't any effort for him to draw her closer and kiss her, firmly, masterfully.

The door to Danny's room opened. He heard Dad
and Mom come in, and pretended for a minute that
he was asleep.

"He's been napping all day," Mom was saying. "He
hardly woke up enough to eat breakfast. I guess he
must have lain awake late last night. But his fever
was down, and he didn't seem restless, so I didn't
call you."

"We'll see how he is now," Dad's voice answered;
and Danny, who had closed his eyes to try to remember better, opened them again.

Dad was bending over his bed.

"How do you feel, son?" he asked.

"I feel swell," Danny told him, and struggled to a
sitting position. "Look what I found yesterday in my
box. What is it, Dad?"

Doctor Norcross took the piece of ivory Danny held
out, and looked at it.

"I'll be darned!" he exclaimed to his wife. "Danny's
found the old Chinese talisman Grandfather Jonas
brought back on the last voyage of the *Yankee Star*.
He gave it to me thirty years ago. Told me it had
belonged to a Chinese magician.

"Its peculiar power, he said, was that if you held it
tight, you could have one wish come true, providing
—as the Chinese inscription on the bottom says—your
mind was pure, your spirit innocent, and your motive
unselfish.

"I wished on it dozens of times, but nothing ever
happened. Guess it was because I was too materialistic
and wished for bicycles and things.

"Here, Danny, you can keep it. But take good care of it. It's very old; even the man who gave it to Grandfather Jonas didn't know how old it was."

Danny took back the talisman.

"I made a wish, Dad," he confessed.

"So?" Dad grinned. "Did it come true?"

"I don't know," Danny admitted. "I can't remember what it was."

Dad chuckled.

"Then I guess it didn't come true," he remarked. "Never mind; you can make another. And if that one doesn't happen either, don't fret. You can keep the talisman and tell people the story. It's a good story, even if it isn't so."

Probably it wasn't so. It was certain that the next time Danny wished, nothing happened. Nor any of the times after that. So that by and by he gave up trying.

He was always a little sorry, though, that he never could remember that first wish, made when he was almost asleep.

But he never could. Not even later, when he heard people remarking how much marriage had improved Alice Wilson's appearance and how silvery Mrs. Bob Morrow's voice was.

Don't Be a Goose

PROFESSOR ALEXANDER PEABODY, with his sister Martha's final emphatic words still ringing in his ears, opened his eyes and blinked at the strange landscape about him. For a moment he felt dizzy, and his head buzzed, with Martha's blunt admonition, "Don't be a goose, Alexander!" seeming to echo through the buzzing.

But some unpleasant symptoms were to be expected. After all, his personality had just hurtled a gap of hundreds of years and taken up temporary abode in a strange body. Such a violent shifting about of the essential ego could not be accomplished without a certain amount of stress and strain.

Gradually the buzzing ceased, the dizziness passed away, and Alexander Peabody, his eyes glistening with excitement, began to examine the details of his surroundings.

He seemed to be sitting on the grassy bank of a small pond, about which grew rushes of unusual height, since they reached well above his head. Beyond them stood a line of curious trees. They were twisted and gnarled, and bore glossy green leaves, but their height astonished him. If they had not been so tall, he would have called them olive trees. But olive trees eighty feet high—— No, they must be some new species.

Professor Peabody started to rise from his sitting position, but quickly sat down again. His legs felt odd. All the muscles of his body seemed strange and uncoördinated. And the movement had brought back the dizziness.

That, no doubt, was due to the fact his personality was not yet adjusted to the new body it had taken. Professor Peabody decided to wait for a few moments, until he became a little better integrated, before starting out to explore his surroundings.

There was, after all, no tremendous hurry. It had taken him twenty years of preparation, since he had found that rare magical spell in a very old book, to reach this moment, and if it had not been for Martha's sarcasm, he might not even yet have summoned up the courage to take the plunge.

But for Martha to laugh and tell him not to be a goose when he had told her that he was tired of teaching physics in an obscure college, and that he had determined to experience at least once in his life danger, adventure, excitement, and perhaps romance —that had been galling in the extreme.

Martha's incredulity had come out in those scornful

words when he had added that the great, secret yearning of his existence was to affect the course of history in some manner, however slightly.

"Don't be a goose, Alexander!" she had exclaimed. "History isn't made by men like you!"

And she had gone out, slamming the door to his study, before he could even explain his plans.

There was no doubt, Professor Peabody thought—tentatively twisting his head and finding that the dizziness was almost gone—that she was partially right. He was small and unimpressive, with a baldish head, horn-rimmed spectacles, a long, thin neck, and a somewhat receding chin.

But he had never intended to try to affect the course of history in the age in which he lived. His plan, if Martha had only waited to hear it, was to return to an earlier era, when his knowledge, intelligence, and general abilities would loom far larger than they did in the twentieth century.

He could do it. Once, at least. And if Martha had only listened, he could have given her the gist of the magical spell which, after twenty years of work, he had mastered: he could force his personality back through the time-pressure of vanished centuries into some corporeal body that had lived long ago.

But Martha had not waited to hear.

"After all, Martha," Alexander Peabody had said with quiet dignity, "I seem to remember that another Alexander made history once."

But he had said it to a closed door. Perhaps it was just as well. If Martha had stayed, there was no telling what she might have retorted.

The proof, after all, was that, smarting under the
sting of her words, he had gone ahead with his plans
and—here he was!

Professor Peabody opened his eyes wide, blinking.
In the momentary confusion of those first few minutes,
he had quite forgotten to wonder *where* he was, in
what land he found himself. And for that matter, in
what century, what year. He chuckled to himself at
the realization. Certainly, before he could plan any
moves, he must know those two things.

And a third, equally important. The identity of the
body in which his ego now——

Alexander Peabody, glancing down at himself automatically, ceased thinking with horrid abruptness. And
his brain reeled in a wild dizziness a dozen times worse
than it had before.

He was—he was covered with white feathers!

Professor Peabody shuddered and closed his eyes,
keeping them shut lest the dizziness that rocked him
unnerve him completely. In heaven's name, what—
what——

Then he was startled by a lilting, feminine voice.

"Hello, handsome," it said. "What're you doing 'way
off here all by your lonesome? How about coming for
a swim? I know a place where we can get some dandy
mud worms."

Alexander Peabody's eyes remained shut. He did not
want to be impolite, but the unknown female would
have to wait for an answer until he felt less giddy.
Besides, in his present distress he certainly didn't want

to go swimming, and mud worms were the last things he could have desired.

Some corner of Alexander Peabody's reeling brain found itself wondering, however, what language the girl was speaking. He had prepared himself for his great adventure by learning Old English, Old French, Latin, and Sanskrit, and he knew that the curiously harsh, hissing tongue that she spoke was none of these.

"Okay, stuck-up!" the girl spoke again. "Don't answer. Sit there and moult, for all I care!"

Professor Peabody heard a splashing in the pond, and opened his eyes. But there was no girl to be seen. There was no one and nothing, save a large white swan swimming away across the little lake, her tail seeming to express disdain.

No, not a swan, though she looked big enough to be one. A—a goose. And—and—it could only have been she who had told him to "sit there and moult."

"Great heavens!" Professor Peabody groaned aloud, his voice harsh and strange in his ears. "Then I *am* a—a——"

He could not say it. But he did not have to. The goose had been talking to him because *he* was a goose, too!

Something of wild despair rang in Alexander Peabody's brain. He had set out to find adventure, to know romance, to affect history; and he had wound up as a barnyard fowl!

His sister Martha was to blame, of course. With those last scornful words, she had set up some psychic channel which must have led him, when he completed the old spell, into this feathered body.

He would have wept, if a goose had been capable of tears; would have sobbed aloud, if a goose could cry.

Then, bit by bit, he got a grip on himself. He was not an uncourageous man—goose, rather. Handicapped he was, but perhaps all was not lost. In any event, it behooved him to learn what he could of this time and country in which he found himself.

With that decision, he rose and started for the water. He settled comfortably down upon the surface of the pond, and found natural instincts enabling him to swim with ease.

Floating thus on the surface, he arched his neck and found that he could examine his appearance by staring at the inverted reflection of himself.

He was, undeniably, a goose. But he gained a crumb of comfort from the fact he was a large goose, a handsome one, with a long, flexible neck; a large, well-shaped head; bright eyes, with a curious dark ring about them, as if he wore spectacles; and a sturdy, well-muscled body.

Experimentally he flapped his wings. Though he did not rise from the water, the effort made him move with good speed across the pond. Swiftly enough, in fact, to overtake the goose that had spoken to him.

Alexander Peabody found himself hurrying after her as she swam toward a small stream. He even found himself admiring her, in a way. She was young, streamlined, a pure dazzling white, with a coquettish flirt to her tail. And she had called him handsome.

It was a new experience to Alexander Peabody to

be called handsome, and even coming from a goose
it was pleasant. It might be entertaining to converse
with her . . .

Professor Peabody coughed—or tried to—abruptly.
Obviously a strong residue of personality remained in
the feathered body he now inhabited. His thoughts
seemed to be part human and part goose. He must
not let himself become confused. It was absurd to
think of himself, Alexander Peabody, B.S., M.S., and
Ph.D., admiring a barnyard fowl. However, she might
be a source of much-needed information.

A moment later he drew alongside her and slowed.
"Er," he began. "That is—ah—good afternoon."

It was remarkably difficult to think what to say to
a goose, and his initial effort drew no response. Professor Peabody tried again.

"I—that is, I hope I wasn't rude just now," he said.

His companion tossed her head, and he caught her
peering at him from the corners of small, bright eyes.
Still she said nothing.

"The truth is," Peabody continued, "I was a bit
dizzy, and I had my eyes closed till the dizziness went
away."

"Oh, that's all right," Miss Goose said now, evidently
considering his apology humble enough. "I know how
it is. You can call me Edna."

"Ah—Edna," Professor Peabody repeated. "A pretty
name. But I was wondering, Miss—er, Edna, if you
could tell me the date."

"Date?" Edna looked at him in puzzlement.

"I mean, what year is it?"

"Year? What is a year?"

"Uh—that is, it doesn't matter," Professor Peabody answered. Naturally, a goose could be expected to know nothing of time. "But perhaps you can tell me where we are, though?"

"Where?" Edna glanced at him sidewise. "Why, here, of course."

"Yes, quite so," Professor Peabody agreed, a little desperate. "But where is 'here'? I mean, what is the name of the place?"

"Name?" Edna said. "It hasn't any name. It's just here. There are only two places—here, and there. And we're here."

"Thank you." Peabody sighed: as nearly a sigh as he could manage. "To be sure. May I also inquire where this stream upon which we are now swimming takes us?"

"How you do talk!" Edna exclaimed, pleased. "I never heard language like you use before. Why, it takes us to the river. Where the people are."

"Ah!" Peabody brightened. "The river. And people. You don't know their names, do you?"

Edna shook her head, her lissome neck undulating pleasantly. "Do people have names?"

"Yes," Alexander Peabody told her as a bend in the stream brought into view a town.

It was not a very imposing town, being merely a largish aggregation of stone and wood houses on the edge of the river into which the stream flowed. But beyond it, on the crest of a hill, was a more imposing structure, almost a fortress, with stout stone walls.

Within the confines of this stronghold Professor Peabody glimpsed the tops of buildings, and he caught sight of human beings on the walls, scanning the horizon in the manner of sentinels.

"What is that?" he asked eagerly, and Edna looked toward the town.

"That's just home," she said. "It's sort of dull. Nothing ever happens there. I just came out for a swim, and because I was hungry for some mud worms. Would you like some? I know a dandy place to get them."

"No, thank you," Alexander Peabody replied hastily. "I—uh, I'd like very much to see where you live."

"Would you?" Edna seemed pleased. "Then come along. What is your name anyway, good-looking?"

"Call me Alex," Professor Peabody suggested.

"Alex. I like that name," Edna told him. "It's a good name for a big, strong fellow like you. All right, Alex. We swim down to that dead tree, then we go up the path, and there's a hole in the wall . . ."

Forty minutes later, Professor Peabody squeezed through a crevice in the stone wall of the fortress and found himself inside. The route Edna had led him had taken them near no human beings. But now there were plenty of people in sight. There were numerous buildings of stone within the walls, and a large one in the center was really very imposing, with lofty pillars and broad marble steps.

The streets were muddy, and filled with refuse, but no one seemed to mind. Individuals strode along about their business, skirting the worst puddles and giving no heed to the garbage.

A short distance away was what seemed to be a market. Nothing was for sale, however, save a few carcasses of small animals. These were being bought by housewives in loose white gowns amidst much bargaining.

All the men in sight were armed, either with swords, or pikes, or both. All wore tunics of white cotton or homespun, and most had leather jerkins or at least leather straps outside these, from which shields were suspended. Professor Peabody realized that he should be able to tell from the dress of the inhabitants where he was. But he couldn't. He was, after all, a scientist, and not a historian. Though something struck a familiar note in his mind, he could not place it.

However, he must somehow make contact with them, and let them know that the body of the fowl he now wore concealed a human soul and mentality.

He was turning his next move over in his mind when he observed a large white fowl approaching him and Edna. It was another goose, a male goose, in fact, and it waddled toward them with an arrogance that Alexander Peabody found distasteful.

"Why, it's Carl!" Edna exclaimed, with a little hiss of interest. "Dear me, Alex, I should warn you: Carl is very fond of me."

"He is, is he?" Professor Peabody responded, finding, to his own amazement, that there was a distinctly ominous tone in his voice.

"Hello, Edna," the oncoming Carl hissed. "Where'd you pick up that mangy-looking bird with you?"

"He's a gentleman friend of mine," Edna answered, with a toss of her head. "We've just been having a little walk together."

"You have, have you?" Carl fixed a beady eye on Alexander Peabody. "Well, tell him to take another walk, before I kick his feathers off."

"Huh!" Edna answered, provocatively. "I guess he can take care of himself. Can't you, Alex?"

"Eh?" Alexander Peabody felt a certain alarm. Carl's intentions were obviously hostile. And despite the curious urge within him to reciprocate that hostility, Professor Peabody was after all a man of peace, who had never engaged in a conflict in his life. "Why— why——"

Carl gave him no chance to make up his mind. Hissing and clacking, Carl charged.

Carl was large, and obviously of a bellicose nature. His first rush knocked the professor off his feet. While he lay on his side, beating his wings and giving out cries of distress, Carl plucked large handfuls of feathers from his anatomy. Then with his powerful beak he nipped Peabody in numerous places, all of which hurt.

Ruffled and flustered, Peabody scrambled to his feet and attempted to strike back. But he was un- accustomed to combat, and Carl bore down on him in so fearsome a manner that the professor's courage gave way. He turned and fled.

As he squawked down the street, feathers flying, wings beating, Carl took a few last nips. Then he ceased, to return to Edna.

"There he goes," Peabody heard his rival hissing

behind him. "You won't see that bird again, bright
eyes."

The professor turned a corner, and skidded to a
wobbly stop as he almost ran into the legs of a man
hurrying toward a flight of marble steps. At first he'd
thought it was a woman, because of the white draperies
fluttering about the sandaled feet.

But the harsh voice that spoke was distinctly mascu-
line, and what it said was, "Be gone from my path,
bird, before I kick you loose from your giblets! On
my word, if you weren't sacred to Minerva, I'd wring
your neck and pop you into the cooking pot, or my
name's not Marcus Manlius!"

A glow of excitement overspread Professor Peabody
even as he fluttered to one side. The language was
Latin. And he must be—yes, the hill and river made
it positive. He was in Rome.

Exultation flamed in Peabody's breast. Rome! At an
early date, obviously, for the place was not much more
than a provincial village. But Rome, where most of
the world's history was made for a thousand years!

He must communicate with the inhabitants quickly,
learn the date, discover into just what stage of Rome's
history he had been precipitated. Then, having all the
facts, he could put his brain and intelligence to work;
and handicapped though he was by the body of a
goose, he might yet triumph over his misfortune.

He scuttled up the muddy steps and got ahead of
the ascending man. The fellow strode with the air
of a commander.

Professor Peabody summoned his best Latin.

"*Hic, haec, hoc!*" he shrilled at the glowering Marcus Manlius, to get his attention. "*Gallia est omnis divisa in partes tres!* Listen, please! I am a friend. It's all a mistake that I look like a goose. I must talk to you!"

To Professor Peabody, waiting expectantly, the purest of Latin seemed to have tripped off his tongue. But the togaed one only glowered.

"Cease, fowl, your hissing and clacking!" he roared at Professor Peabody. "By the gods, you make my ears ring! If it weren't for the blessed Minerva's protection, I'd break you into seventy-seven bits. Now, out of my way!"

Dismayed, Professor Peabody tried to scuttle aside. He was too slow. A foot caught just beneath the tail feathers. He sailed through the air and down the steps.

Gasping for breath, Professor Peabody spread his wings, flapping furiously. But unacquainted as he was with the art of flight, something went wrong. He went into a side slip, then into a stall, and in getting out of that, into a tailspin. A moment later he made a landing on the bottom step that jarred all remaining breath from his body.

On the steps above, harsh laughter sounded. Then Marcus Manlius was gone.

Slowly Professor Peabody recovered his breath, his wits, and his courage. He had failed to make the man understand. Probably his accent had been wrong. Or more likely, his vocal cords were not adapted to clear reproduction of human speech.

Yet somehow he must communicate with the Romans, or twenty years of labor and a lifetime of ambition were gone for nothing.

It was a problem requiring the utmost concentration. He decided to stroll about the town while he pondered it. Besides, he did not feel like sitting down. Not just now.

Slowly and with dignity, Professor Peabody proceeded down the muddy lane that served for a street. From the corner of his eye he saw Edna and Carl strolling in the other direction. For a moment a flush of humiliation flooded Peabody. Then, putting trivial personal matters from his mind, he concentrated on how to communicate with the Romans.

Presently his eyes brightened. Seated on a doorstep ahead of him, to get the last light of the afternoon, was an individual marking on parchment with a quill pen, which he dipped now and again into a pot of ink beside him.

Hope rose in Professor Peabody. This was a scribe, an educated man. He approached cautiously. The intent scribe, a scrawny fellow with a bald spot in the middle of his pate, took no notice of him. Peabody went closer.

If, he thought, he could take the quill pen in his mouth—his beak, rather—and write a message with it—— No, that was impractical. But still——

He cleared his throat. He'd try speech again first. He did, uttering a few preliminary sentences, but the scribe only glanced up in annoyance.

"Shoo!" he said. "Get hence, bird. No, pause a moment!"

Alexander Peabody, having started back, stopped. The scribe's expression was more friendly. Taking heart at this sign of interest, Peabody bent his neck, inserted his beak into the smooth mud beside the doorstep, and began to make awkward capital letters.

"H-I-C," he wrote, sprawlingly but plainly. "H-A-E-C . . . H-O-C."

Triumphantly he stood back. There! That would demonstrate he was intelligent. Get the scribe's attention. Then he would write a real sentence. Then——

He looked up. The scribe made a swift grab at him. A large hand seized his wing. Pain shot through Professor Peabody. He leaped forward, straight between the fellow's legs. His wings flapping, he shot into the clear, and behind him the scribe tottered, grabbed at air, and sat down with a resounding smack in the mud —fair on the words Alexander Peabody had written!

Peabody groaned. The furious writer was struggling to his feet with a handful of feathers and a stone. He hurled the stone. Peabody dodged around a corner.

Confound the fellow! He had only wanted some feathers to make new goose quill pens. Using him, Professor Alexander Peabody, B.S., M.S., Ph.D., as a source of writing materials!

Then Peabody's neck sagged, his tail feathers drooped. Evening was coming on, and a cold, raw wind was whisking through the streets of Rome. He'd failed to communicate with anyone, and gloomily he

could see that no matter what he tried, he'd fail again.
Who would pay any attention to a goose?

He sighed, and then a determination crystallized.
He'd go back, and see Edna again. Maybe she was
just a goose, but she was company, someone to talk
to, and he was lonely.

As for Carl, if he could find him now, he'd thrash
him to within an inch of his life!

He turned about, and went in search of Edna and
Carl.

A curious thing was happening to Alexander Peabody, and he was only half aware of it. The residue
of goosish personality in the body his ego was in-
habiting seemed to be coloring his thoughts and
actions. He was gradually losing interest in human
affairs, even in the mission which had brought him
here.

Conversely, the more he thought of Edna, the more
he desired her company. The more he thought of the
uncouth Carl, the more he desired a chance to engage
him in combat again, to beak-whip him until his pin-
feathers came loose.

In a highly bellicose state of mind, Professor Alexander Peabody waddled down the muddy streets of
Rome, ruffling his feathers.

But he could not find Carl and Edna, and night
had come on. He began to be hungry. He found a
crust dropped beside a doorway, and his beak broke
it up into crumbs. He swallowed them, washing them
down with water from a puddle, and felt refreshed.

Now, however, in the darkness he was quite lost.

The town had gone to bed shortly after nightfall. Occasionally a cloaked figure, sword at his side, shield slung over his back, passed. These seemed to be sentries, for Professor Peabody saw them take up places at the walls.

But as the night wore on, and the raw wind grew keener, he saw the sentries leaving their exposed positions and seeking protected niches where they might keep warm. Peabody, however, was not interested in them. A wan moon was rising, and down the street he could now see the temple outside which he had parted from Carl and Edna.

He hastened toward it.

And there they were, crouched cozily side by side in a corner, behind a fluted column, sleeping with their wings touching.

Indignation and jealousy made Professor Peabody emit a hiss of rage that brought the two sleepers to startled wakefulness. Then Edna blinked coyly.

"Why, it's Alex!" she said.

"Listen, you bag of feathers," Carl clacked, "beat it, or I'll pull you wing from wing."

"You and who else?" Peabody retorted, remembering in time a favorite answer of youth to such challenges. "You pusillanimous fowl, I'll beat you down into goose grease!"

"Oh, Alex!" Edna sighed. "What lovely language you use! And how handsome you are when you're angry!"

"Take a last look at him then, bright-eyes," Carl told her. "Because when I finish with him, he won't have enough feathers left to cover a sparrow."

And he rushed to the attack.

Professor Peabody gave way at first, mainly because he wanted the combat to take place on a different field of honor—the flat surface beyond the temple. The marble of Minerva's temple was slippery, and he wanted firm footing for this chivalric joust in which he was engaged.

So he scurried backwards and down the far steps, into the vacant lot where the rising moon gave a clear if subdued light. Carl pursued, hissing in triumph, and the sound of battle brought scores of sleepy geese running after them from the corners of the temple.

In the middle of the open space, Professor Peabody took his stand. He stopped running and began to attack.

The change in tactics took Carl by surprise, and Professor Peabody got in half a dozen sound, smacking beak-blows to the head. Then Carl screamed in redoubled rage and closed with him.

The other geese gathered about to watch, hissing in shrill excitement. Above all the voices, though, Edna's could be heard most clearly, and her "Oh, Alex, don't let him hurt you!" was sweet music to Professor Peabody's ears.

Professor Peabody, however, for all his valor, was unversed in the best fighting strategy of the fowl world. He was slowly getting the worst of the terrific wing-to-wing, beak-to-beak tussle when an interruption occurred. A torch flared near by, and a voice which he recognized roared in terrible rage.

"By the sacred bones of my ancestors, I'll slice the

gizzard from the goose with the black marking around
its eyes, Minerva or no Minerva! Today on the Forum
steps it made my ears ache with its hissing, and tonight
it must engage in battle and make the air hideous
noise, waking honest Romans from their needful sleep.
I'll toast its liver and grill its gizzard and stew its
bones and——"

Another voice cut the first short.

"Marcus Manlius! They come. The enemy come
stealing up the hillside path!"

Then indeed did the night become sonorous with
the sound of battle. Men rushed forth into the street,
buckling on shields and short swords. Torches flared
bright. From the city wall came shrill barbaric war
cries, the gasp and scream of wounded men.

But Alexander Peabody heeded it not. He had his
own fight to attend to. Carl was still strong and fresh,
and pressing him back. So Peabody, in desperation,
altered his tactics.

His new fighting method was a combination of all
he could recall of the best features of chivalric jousting
by knights with lances, and modern pursuit plane dog-
fighting. Extending his neck like a spear, he rushed
into Carl. His hard beak bored through Carl's defenses
and bowled him over. Following up his advantage,
Professor Peabody took to the air.

With a great flapping of wings, he gained an altitude
of three feet, and from there dive-bombed Carl. Carl,
struggling up, received all of Peabody's weight on the
side of his head and went down again, stunned. Alexander Peabody, withdrawing a yard or so, rushed in

once more with the leveled spear technique.

Carl gave ground. Professor Peabody pursued. Carl turned and ran for safety, and Peabody delivered one last triumphant blow. Then Carl's agonized squawks were receding down the street into the night, and Edna was snuggling up to Alexander Peabody as he leaned against the temple steps, panting for breath.

"Alex," Edna said, "you were *wonderful*." And she rubbed her long, lissome white neck against his.

A strange thrill warmed Professor Peabody's blood. He had conquered an enemy in combat, and he had won the admiration of a fair lady.

"It wasn't anything really, Edna," he said modestly. "That Carl, he's just an over-rated bully."

"It *was* something," Edna breathed. "You're a hero, Alex. Anyway, you're *my* hero."

"It was for you I did it," Alexander Peabody said boldly. "And I'll always fight for you if—if you'll let me."

"Oh, Alex!" Edna sighed, and pressed close against him.

They were alone, the other geese having gone back to sleep. And in his absorption, Professor Peabody was quite deaf to the diminishing sound of fighting at the city's walls. It was not until some time later when the light of torches came toward them, making him blink, that he remembered the Romans at all.

Then, as he looked up, a burly figure clad in animal skins leaped from the midst of a band of Roman soldiers and, snatching a sword from one, rushed at Professor Peabody.

"We'd have had you, cursed Romans," a bull voice roared in bad Latin, "had it not been for this goose hatched of Satan! I saw him myself, as we were about to charge over the wall, fighting with another to awaken you. And he shall die for it!"

Edna screamed in fright as the huge soldier came at them, sword swinging. But Alexander Peabody felt no fear. He launched himself forward, beak extended, hissing ferociously. He leaped, and struck for the eyes as the glittering blade descended.

One ferocious jab he got in, while behind him Edna's anguished voice cried, *"Alex! Alex!"* Then the edge of the sword met his neck, and Professor Alexander Peabody knew only darkness.

The blackness may have lasted for a minute or an hour. Peabody could not tell. But as it lifted slowly, he heard Edna crying still, "Alex! Alex!" and shaking him by the wing with her beak to arouse him. Professor Peabody opened his eyes, blinking.

"It's all right, Edna," he gasped. "I'm all right. I——"

Then he stopped, for it was his sister Martha he was staring at.

She stepped back, letting go his shoulder, and Alexander Peabody saw that he was in his Morris chair, in his study, and that it was night outside.

"Alexander!" Martha exclaimed. "What has happened? I came in and—and you seemed to be asleep in your chair. But though I shook you for the longest time I couldn't seem to wake you up."

She stopped and stared at him.

"Who is Edna? What has happened to you? You—
you look different."

Alexander Peabody did not answer her immediately.
He rose from the chair, marched to his bookcase, drew
down a volume of the encyclopedia. And there he
found the name he sought. For a moment he stared
at the page.

> **MARCUS MANLIUS CAPITOLINUS.** A patrician.
> Roman consul in 392 B.C. According to tradition,
> when in 390 B.C. the besieging Gauls were attempting
> to scale the walls of the Capitol, he was roused by
> the cackling of the sacred geese, rushed to the spot,
> and threw down the foremost assailants. The attack
> on Rome was defeated.

Slowly Peabody closed the volume and looked up,
to meet Martha's gaze.

"I *am* changed," he proclaimed. "I have known
adventure. I have routed an enemy in single-handed
combat. And I have affected the course of history.

"I am responsible for the fact that the Gauls did
not capture Rome in 390 B.C. If Rome had fallen then,
the Roman Empire might never have been. If the
Roman Empire had not existed, the history of the
world would have been vastly different. So I have
affected history more than any modern dictator can
ever hope to do. I, Alexander Peabody. And I'm
satisfied."

Martha goggled at him. Then gradually she relaxed
and shook her head.

"You've had a dream, I see," she commented. "But don't try to tell me you believe that your dream actually happened. Please don't be a goose."

Alexander Peabody gazed at his sister, not with resentment, but with a bright, faraway look in his eye, as if he were thinking back to some special moment in his life.

"Certainly not, Martha," he replied with dignity. "In any case, you know, I would be a gander."

Do You Believe in Ghosts?

tHIS IS IT," Nick Deene said with enthusiasm after he had stared down at the old Carriday house for a couple of minutes. "This is what I had in mind. Right down to the last rusty hinge and creaking floorboard."

Danny Lomax heaved a sigh of relief.

"Praise be!" he said. "We've wasted almost a week finding a house that suited you just right, and that doesn't leave us much time to start the publicity. Although I'll admit"—Danny squinted down at the brooding old pile of stone and lumber that still retained some traces of a one-time dignity—"I'll admit you've really turned up a honey. If that isn't a haunted house, it'll do until one comes along."

Nick Deene stood for a moment longer, appraising the Carriday mansion, on whose arched entrance the carved figure 1784 still defied the corroding elements.

The building was a long, L-shaped Colonial-type house, with stone foundations and hand-sawed clap-board upper structure. It had been painted some dark color once, but the color had gone with the years, leaving the structure a scabrous, mottled hue.

The building was two-storied, with attics, and seemed to contain a number of rooms. Woods, once cut back, had crept up almost to the walls and gave the place a cramped, crowded feeling. A weed-grown dirt carriage drive connecting with a half-impassable county road, and the tumbled ruins of a couple of outbuildings, finished off the scene.

"It has everything, Danny!" Nick Deene went on, with animation. "Absolutely everything but a ghost."

"Which is just fine with me," asserted the technical assistant allotted him by his radio hour sponsors—*So-Pure Soaps present Dare Danger with Deene!* "Of course, I don't believe in ghosts, as the hill-billy said about the hippopotamus, but that's all the more reason I don't want to go meeting one. I'm too old to go around revising my beliefs just to please a spook."

"That's just it," Nick Deene told him. "A resident ha'nt that somebody or other had seen, or thought he'd seen, and described, would cramp my style. Of course, nobody comes out here, and it's spooky enough to make any casual passer-by take another road, but there's no definite legend attached to it. That's what I've been looking for—that, plus a proper background. And this has the proper background. Three genera-tions of Carridays died here—of malaria, probably; look at the swamp back there. The last Carriday ran away to sea and died in Java. The place has been empty fifteen years now, except for a tramp found in it one winter, dead of pneumonia. Nobody's going to buy it, not away out here in a swampy section of woods. For a couple thousand dollars the estate agent will be glad enough to let us have the key and do anything we want to it, including furnishing it with a nice, brand-new ghost. Which is just what I'm going to do."

"Nicholas Deene, Hand-Tailored Spooks, Ghost Maker to the Nobility," Danny Lomax grunted. "You know, I used to read your books and believe 'em. That chapter where you told about the doomed dancing girl in the old temple at Anghor Vat, and how you saved her just before the priests came for her, gave me a big kick once. I was young enough to think it had really happened!"

"Well, there *is* a temple at Anghor Vat." Nick Deene grinned. "And dancing girls too. So if you enjoyed the story, why complain? You believed it when you read it, didn't you?"

"Yeah," Danny Lomax agreed, stamping out a cigarette. "I believed it."

"Then you got your money's worth," the tall, bronzed man asserted. (Sun lamp treatments every evening, carefully timed by his valet, Walters, kept that bronze in good repair.) "And a million people still believe that story. Just as ten million people are going to believe in the Carriday Curse."

"All right," the small, wiry man assented. "I'm not here to argue. Even if the Carriday Curse is strictly a Nick Deene fake, I don't like this place. If I had a lot of baby spooks I wanted to raise, I'd bring 'em here and plant 'em. The atmosphere is so unhealthy!"

Nick Deene smiled the flashing toothed smile that had won him indulgence all around the globe, had been photographed against the columns of the Athenaeum, halfway up Mount Everest, atop an elephant going over the Alps, and too many other places to list. He brushed back the jet-black hair that lay so smoothly against his skull, and started back toward the road. Danny Lomax followed, making plans out loud.

"We can have '_m run a mobile unit up to the road, here," he decided. "You'll have a portable sender on your back, and the unit will pick it up and retransmit to Hartford. Hartford will pipe it into New York and out through the network. We'll give the equipment a thorough check so there's not much chance of anything going wrong. Your rating has been falling off lately, but this'll hypo the box office up to the top again. Most of your listeners have already read the stuff you've been dramatizing on the ether, you know. This one, a direct broadcast from a haunted house on the night of Friday the 13th, will pull 'em in. You're a fake, Deene, but you got some good ideas, and this is one of the better ones. *If.*"

"If what?" Nick demanded challengingly, as they reached the road and prepared to clamber into a waiting car.

"If you put it over." Danny Lomax took the right-hand seat and slammed the door. "A lot of newspaper men don't like you any too well, and if there's any stink to this thing they'll horse-laugh it to death. There has to be a ghost, and your audience has to believe in it. Don't make any mistake about that."

"There'll be a ghost," Nick Deene shrugged, putting the car into motion. "And they'll believe in it. I'll be right in the room with 'em. I'm working on the script now. I'm going to ask them to turn out the light when they listen, and imagine they're with me, waiting in the dark for the Thing that for a hundred years has been the Curse of the Carridays to appear. I'll be armed only with a flashlight, a Bible, and——"

"And a contract," Danny interrupted. "Sorry. But I've lost all my illusions since meeting you."

"And a crucifix," Deene continued, a little nettled by now. "They'll hear boards creaking, and a death-watch beetle ticking in the wall. And plenty of other details. I'll make them up as I go along. Spontaneity always gives the most convincing effect, I've found. And they'll be convinced. Aren't they always?"

"Yes," the advertising man agreed reluctantly. "When you go into your act, old ladies swoon with excitement and little kids scream all night in their cribs. There was one heart-failure—an old maid in Dubuque—after last month's show, the one in which you were fighting an octopus forty feet beneath the surface, down in the Malay pearling waters."

"There'll be half a dozen this time," Nick Deene prophesied complacently. "When I start into the Carriday house to meet the Thing with a face like an oyster——"

"A face like an oyster, huh?" Danny Lomax repeated,

and swallowed hard. "That's what it's going to look like?"

Nick Deene chuckled and nodded.

"If there's anything deader looking than a watery blue oyster that's been open too long," he said, "I don't know what it is. Where was I? Oh, yes. Well, when I start into that house to wait for the approach of the Thing with an oyster face, I'm going to scare the living daylights out of ten million people, if you guys do your jobs right."

"We will, we will," Danny promised. "We'll ship out photos of the house, I'll plant the story the locals should repeat to a couple of fellows in the village, we'll ballyhoo you all the way down the line. The only thing we won't do is try to fix the weatherman to make it a stormy night. You'll have to take your chances on that."

"It's generally foggy down here in the swamps at night," Deene replied, quite seriously. "Fog is as good as a storm any time."

"Yeah," Danny Lomax agreed, twisting around to look down at the house in the hollow below—the road having taken them up a slope behind it. Fog was already forming in tenuous gray wisps, as the disappearance of the sun brought cool air currents rolling down into the swampy dell. "Fog's good enough for me, any time. You know, Deene, maybe it's a good thing you don't believe in spooks yourself."

"Maybe it is, at that." Nick Deene grinned as they topped a rise and the Carriday house disappeared from view.

It was not a foggy night. Yet there were mists about the Carriday house as Danny Lomax, Nicholas Deene, and two newspaper men—Ken Blake and Larry Miller —prepared to enter it.

Sitting as it did in the very bottom of a little glen, it was wrapped in pale vapor that danced and shifted in slow, stately movements. A quarter moon thrust a weak finger of radiance down into the woods. It was eleven o'clock, and time for *Dare Danger With Deene* to hit the air with its special broadcast.

Danny Lomax had earphones clamped to his ears, tentacles of wire trailing back from them to the broadcast unit pulled up beside the road. The house was four hundred yards away, and Danny was conscious of a vague regret it wasn't four million as he snatched off the earphones and dropped his hand.

Nick Deene caught the signal, which meant that the theme music was finished, as well as the lengthy announcement outlining the circumstances of the broadcast. His deep, expressive voice took up the tale without a hitch.

"This is Nicholas Deene speaking," he said easily into the mike attached to his chest and connected to the pack broadcaster slung over his shoulder. "The old Carriday mansion lies in a depression below me, some four hundred yards away. Wan moonlight illuminates it. Veils of fog wrap around it as if to hide it from man's gaze. For fifteen years no human being has spent a night beneath its roof—alive."

His voice paused significantly, to let his unseen

audience experience its first prickle of pleasurable terror.

"But tonight I am going to brave the curse of the Carridays. I am going to enter the house. And in the great master bedroom where three generations of Carridays died, I am going to wait for the unknown Thing that legends tell of to appear.

"I am going toward the house now, with two reputable newspaper men at my side. One of them has a pair of handcuffs, the other the key. They are going to handcuff me to the sturdy bedposts of the dust-covered ancient four-poster that can be seen through the window in the master bedroom. That is to insure that I shall not leave before midnight strikes—before this ill-omened Friday the thirteenth passes away into the limbo of the vanished days."

Nick Deene's voice went on, rising and falling in carefully cadenced rolls, doing little tricks to the emotions of listeners a mile, a thousand miles, three thousand miles away. He and Danny Lomax and the two reporters trudged on downhill toward the house.

This was a last-minute inspiration of Nick Deene's, this handcuff business. The press had taken a somewhat scoffing note toward the stunt broadcast. But Nick Deene's showman's instinct had risen to the occasion. There was a compellingness to the idea of a man being chained in a deserted house, haunted or not—being unable to leave—which had impressed the critics.

Deene kept on talking as they approached the old

mansion, flashlight beams dancing ahead of them. He described the woods, the night sounds, the dancing mist, the appearance of the empty, silent mansion ahead of them, and did a good job. Not that it was necessary for the three men with him. Even before they reached the house, the carefully cultivated skepticism which Blake and Miller had sported was gone from their faces. Cynical though they were, Danny Lomax thought he could catch traces of uneasiness on their countenances.

"We are standing on the rotten, creaking porch now," Deene was telling his audience. "One reporter is unlocking the door with the key given us reluctantly by the white-haired agent for the property, a man whose expression tells us that he knows many things about this house his closed lips will not reveal.

"The door creaks open. Our lights probe the black throat of the hall. Dust is everywhere, seeming inches thick. It rises and swirls about us as we enter——"

They went in, and Nick Deene's tread was the firmest of the four as they strode the length of a narrow hall and reached the stairs. Their lights showed side rooms, filled with old furniture whose dust covers had not been removed in almost two decades. The stairs were winding, and creaked. The air was as musty as it always is in houses long closed.

They reached the second floor where a finger of moonlight intruded through an end window. Their flashlights reflected off a dusty mirror, and Larry Miller jumped uneasily. Nick Deene chuckled into the microphone, and a million listeners nodded in quick approval of his courage.

"My friends are nervous," Nick Deene was telling them. "They feel the atmosphere that hangs so heavy in these silent rooms trod only by creatures of the unseen.

"But we are now in the bedroom where I shall wait——"

The bedroom was big. The door leading into it, though, was low and narrow, and the windows were small. A broken shutter hanging outside creaked in an unseen air current.

There were two old chairs, a bureau, a cedar chest, a rag rug—and the four-poster bedstead. A coverlet, gray with dust, lay over the mattress. Nick Deene grimaced as he saw it, but his voice did not falter.

Danny Lomax snatched the coverlet off the bed and shook it. Dust filled the air, and he coughed as he put the coverlet back into place. He slid a chair up beside the bed, and Nick Deene, without disturbing the broadcast, slid off his pack transmitter and placed it on the chair.

He lay down on the bed, and Larry Miller, with a pair of handcuffs from his pocket, linked one ankle to the left bedpost. Danny Lomax adjusted the mike so that Nick Deene could speak into it without having to hold it, and Deene waved his hand in a signal of preparedness.

"My friends are preparing to depart," he told his audience. His words leaped from the room to the waiting mobile unit, from there to Hartford, twenty miles away, thence to New York, and then to the world, or whatever part of it might be listening. "In a moment I shall be alone. I have a flashlight, but to conserve the batteries I am going to turn it out.

"May I make a suggestion? Why don't you, who are listening, turn out your lights too, and we will wait together in darkness for the approach of the creature known as the Curse of the Carridays—a creature which I hope, before the next hour is over, to describe to you.

"What it is or what it looks like, I do not know. The one man who could tell—the agent for the property—faithful to his trust though the last Carriday died long since in far-off Java, will not speak. Yet, if the portents are favorable, we—you and I—may see it tonight."

Clever, Danny Lomax thought, his trick of identifying the audience with himself, making them feel as if they were on the spot, too. One of the big secrets of his success.

"Now," Nick Deene was saying, "I take my leave of my companions——"

Then Danny and the two reporters were leaving. Nick Deene kicked his leg, the chain of the handcuff rattled, and Larry Miller jumped. Nick waved a sardonic hand after them.

They went downstairs, not dawdling, and no one spoke until they were outside. Then Blake drew a deep breath.

"He's a phony," he said, with reluctant admiration. "And you know as well as I do that if he sees anything tonight, it'll be strictly the product of his imagination. But just the same, I wouldn't spend an hour in that place, handcuffed to the furniture, for a month's pay."

Without hesitating, they set off for the waiting unit, and the small knot of men—technicians, reporters, and advertising agency men—clustered around it. And as they hurried, lights went out in a house here, another there—in Boston, in Sioux Falls, Kalamazoo, Santa Barbara and a thousand other towns—as some of Nick Deene's farflung audience obeyed his melodramatic suggestion to listen to him in the darkness. And two million families settled themselves to wait with him, hanging on his every word, their acceptance of everything he said complete, their belief utter.

When the three men reached the mobile unit again, the little group of half a dozen men there were clustered about the rear, where a half-circle of light burned through the darkness and a loud-speaker repeated Nick Deene's every word.

Deene was still building atmosphere. His resonant voice was picturing the house, the shadows, the dust, the darkness that seemed to crouch within the hallways.

"Listen," Nick Deene was saying, and Danny Lomax could visualize the big bronzed man grinning sardonically as he spoke, "and hear with me the small night sounds that infest this ancient, spirit-ridden dwelling. Somewhere a board is creaking—perhaps for no tangible cause. I cannot tell. But it comes to me clearly——"

Listening, they could hear it, too. The eerie, chill-provoking creak of a floor board or stairway, in midnight silence. Nick Deene had two bits of wood in his pocket that he rubbed together to get that effect, but only Danny Lomax knew that. And even knowing, he did not like the sound.

"I hear the creaking——" Nick Deene's voice was low, suspense-filled now—— "I hear the creaking, and something else. A monotonous tick-tick-tick that seems to become louder and louder as I listen to it, the frightening beat of the death-watch beetle within the walls of this room——"

They could hear that too, as Nick Deene's voice died out. Hear it, and their own breathing became faster as if they too were in that room, listening with a man bound to the great four-poster there.

And in Atlanta, in Rochester, in Cincinnati, in Memphis, Mobile, Reno, Cheyenne, and a thousand other cities and towns, Nick Deene's listeners heard it too in the hushed silence in which they listened. They swallowed a little harder, looked about them a little uneasily, and smiled—smiles that were palpably artificial. And they believed——

Danny Lomax would have believed, too, if he hadn't known of the small metal contrivance by which Nick Deene managed the "death-watch beetle" noises. Even knowing, he admitted to himself that it was an impressive performance. When Nick Deene had boasted that he would make ten million people believe in the "curse of the Carridays" he had exaggerated—but not about their believing. His audience probably didn't number more than five million. But he had most of that five million by now in a complete state of belief for anything he might want to say next.

Danny glanced at his watch, turning his wrist so

that the timepiece caught the light. Thirty-five minutes
gone. Twenty-five to go. Time now for Deene to start
turning on the heat. Time for the sock punch to start
developing. He'd built up his background and sold his
audience. Now he ought to begin to deliver.

He did. A moment later, Nick Deene's voice paused
abruptly. The sudden silence held more suspense than
any words he could have spoken. It held for ten
seconds, twenty, thirty. Then he broke it only with a
half-whispered announcement.

"I think I can hear something moving outside the
house——"

Around the unit there was utter silence, save for the
hum of the generator that was pumping the broadcast
over the hills and woods to Hartford.

"Whatever it is——" Nick Deene's voice was still
low, still that of a man who whispers an aside even
while intent upon something else—— "whatever it is,
it's coming closer. It seems to be moving slowly up
from the small patch of swamp just south of the house."

Absently, Danny Lomax reached for a cigarette.
Nick was sticking to the general script they'd outlined.
Almost at the last minute, they'd decided against a
spiritual manifestation, a ghost pure and simple.

Instead, with his usual instinct for getting the right
note, Nick Deene had switched to a *Thing*. Something
nameless, something formless, something unclassifiable.
Something out of the night and the swamp and the
unknown. Something that might be alive and might
not be alive. But something that, when Nick Deene
got through describing it, would be very, very real——

"Whatever it is, it's coming closer," Nick Deene reported then. "I hear a dragging, dull sound, as of something heavy moving through dead brush and over rough ground. It may be just an animal, perhaps even a stray cow, or a horse, or a wild pig escaped from a pen somewhere on an adjacent farm——"

Five million listeners held their breath a moment. Of course, just a stray horse, or a cow. Something warm, something familiar, something harmless. Then——

"It's pulling at the boards which cover the cellar windows!" Nick Deene exclaimed. "It's trying to get into the house!"

Danny Lomax held his cigarette unlighted, until the flaring match burned his fingers. In spite of their determined skepticism, there was an intentness to the faces of the reporters and technicians gathered around the end of the mobile unit. They knew or guessed this was a phony. Yet the sudden jolt, after Deene had given their nerves a moment in which to relax, got them all. Just as it was getting the whole great, unseen audience.

Danny Lomax, from years of listening to radio programs behind the scenes, had developed a sixth sense of his own. He could tell almost to a degree just how a program was going over—whether it was smashing home or laying an egg. He could feel the audience that listened reacting, and he could sense what their reactions were.

Now something was pulling at him—something strained and tense and uneasy. Several million people or more were listening, were believing, were living through the scene with Nicholas Deene. Crouched there in the chilly night beside the broadcast unit, Danny Lomax could feel the waves of their belief sweeping past him, impalpable but very real.

Nick Deene's voice had quickened. He was reporting now the sound of nails shrieking as they pulled free, as boards gave way. He described a heavy, squashy body forcing its way through the tiny window. He made his listeners hear the soft, squashy sounds of something large and flabby moving through the darkness of the cellar of the house, finding the stairs, going up them slowly, slowly, slowly——

"Now it's in the hall." The big man's words were short, sharp, electric. "It's coming toward the door. I hear boards creaking beneath its weight. It senses that I'm here. It's searching for me. I confess I'm frightened. No sane man could fail to be. However, I am convinced it can't hurt me. If it's a psychic manifestation, it's harmless, however horrifying its appearance may be. So I am keeping a firm grip on my nerves. Only if they betray me can I be endangered.

"Whatever it is, it's just outside the doorway now. The room is in darkness. The moon has set. I have my flashlight, though, and I am going to turn it full on the thing in the doorway.

"I can smell a musty, damp odor, as of swamps and wet places. It is very strong. Almost overpowering. But now I'm going to turn on the light——"

Nick Deene's voice ceased. Danny Lomax's wrist-watch ticked as loudly as an alarm clock. The seconds passed. Ten. Twenty. Thirty. Forty. Someone shifted position. Someone's breath was rasping like that of a choking sleeper.

Then—— "It's going!" Nick Deene's voice was a whisper. "It looked at me, and would have entered. I could sense what it wished. It wished—*me*. But I have the Bible and crucifix I brought tightly in my hand, the light has been shining full into its—its face, if I can call it that. I did not lower my gaze, and now it's going. I can no longer see it. The light of my flash falls on the black, empty frame of the door-way. *It* is slithering back down the hall, toward the steps. It is returning to the swamp from which it came when it sensed my presence here.

"I can hardly describe it. I don't know what it was. It stood as high as a man, yet its legs were only stumps of grayness without feet of any kind. Its body was long and bulbous, like a misshapen turnip, its flesh grayish and uneven. It shone a little, as if with slime, and I saw droplets of water on it catch the light of my torch.

"It had a head, a great round head that was as hairless as the rest of it. And a face—I cannot make you see it as I saw it. Staring into it, I could only think of an oyster. A monstrous, wet, blue-gray oyster, with two darker spots that must have been eyes.

"It had arms. At least, two masses of matter attached to either side of its body reached out a little toward me. There were no hands on the ends of them. Just strings of—corruption.

"That was all I could see. Then it turned. Now it has gone. It has reached the bottom steps, going down with a shuffling, bumping noise. It is moving toward the cellar stairs, the floor creaking beneath it, back to the cellar window through which it forced itself, back to the depths of the swamp from which it emerged. Yet the sense of it still hangs in this room, and I know that if my will should slacken, it could feel it, and return. But it must not. I will not let it. It *must* return to the bottomless muck from which it came——"

Danny Lomax touched his dry lips with his tongue. This was it. This was the high spot. This was where Nick Deene got over, or fell flat on his face. Danny knew that whichever it was, he'd be able to sense it.

And he did. Not failure. Success! The unseen currents that eddied around him were belief. The belief of millions of people, wrapped in a skein spun of words. The belief of millions of listeners seeing in their minds something that had never existed, but which Nick Deene had created and put there.

Tomorrow they might laugh. They might belittle and ridicule the very fact that they had listened. But they'd never be able to forget how they had felt. And now, for the moment at least, they believed. Completely.

Danny let out a breath, and looked at his watch. Almost midnight. Nick Deene was speaking again.

"It's gone now. It's outside again, seeking the swamp from which it came. This is Nicholas Deene speaking. I'm going to sign off now. I've been through quite a nerve strain. Thanks for listening, everybody. I'm glad that you weren't disappointed, that something happened tonight to make this broadcast worth your listening. Good night, all. This is Nicholas Deene saying good night."

Danny Lomax saw the chief engineer throw a switch, and nod to him. He leaned forward toward a secondary mike in the unit, and slipped on a pair of headphones.

"All right, Nick," he said. "You're off the air. We're coming down to unlock you now."

"Okay," Nick Deene's voice came back, a little ragged. "Hurry, will you? The last couple of minutes, I could swear I *have* heard noises outside. Maybe I'm too good. I'm believing myself. How'd it go?"

"Went fine," Danny told him. "They ate it up. Five million people are sitting in their parlors this minute, getting the stiffness out of their muscles, and trying to pretend they didn't believe you."

"I told you they would." Deene's voice was momentarily complacent. Then it became edged again. "Listen, hurry, will you? There *is* something moving around outside this house—— You say they ate it up?"

"Straight," Danny Lomax told him. "I could feel it. They're all still seeing that Thing you described, with the oyster face, crawling in through the cellar window, slithering up the stairs, standing in your doorway——"

"Cut it!" Deene ordered abruptly. "And come down here. *There's something coming in the cellar window where we loosened the boards for the reporters to find!*"

Lomax turned.

"Oh, Joe," he called to the driver. "Take the unit down in front of the house, will you? Save walking. . . . What did you say then, Nick? I missed it."

"I said there's something coming in the cellar window!" Nick Deene's voice was almost shrill. "It's knocking around in the cellar. It's coming toward the stairs!"

"Steady, Nick, steady," Danny Lomax cautioned. "Don't let your nerves go now. You and I know it's just a gag. Don't go and——"

"Good grief!" Deene's breath was coming in gasps. *"There's something coming up the stairs!* Come and get me out of here!"

Danny looked up, a frown between his eyes.

"Joe, get going, will you?" he snapped, and the driver looked around in annoyed surprise.

"Right away," he grunted, and the unit jerked forward. "This fast enough to suit you?"

Danny Lomax didn't answer.

"Nick, you all right?" he demanded of the mike, and Deene's voice, almost unrecognizable, came back.

"Danny, Danny," it gobbled, "there's something coming up the stairs with a sort of thump-thump. I can smell marsh gas and ammonia. There's something making a slithery sound. *I tell you something has got into this house from the swamp and is after me!"*

The unit was jolting down the long unused road. The reporters had swung on. They were staring at Danny, sensing something, they didn't know what, going wrong. Danny, the earphones tight, hung over the mike.

"Take it easy, take it easy," he soothed. "We wrote all that down. It's just on paper. You just said it. Five million people believed it, but you and I don't have to, Nick. We——"

"Listen to me!" Nick cried. "There's something in the hall. Something that scrapes and thumps. The floorboards are creaking. Danny, you know I'm chained here. It's coming after me. It is! It is!" Nick Deene's voice was hysterical. "It's at the doorway. It's——"

The voice was drowned out by a scraping of gravel as the brakes went on abruptly. Wheels fought for traction, lost it. A muddy spot had slewed the broadcast unit to one side. The long-untended road gave no hold. The rear wheels slid toward the ditch beside the road. The unit jolted, toppled, was caught as the hubs dug into a clay bank. The newspaper men were jolted off. Danny Lomax was bounced away from the mike, his earphones torn off his head.

He scrambled back toward the mike. The earphones were cracked. He threw a switch cutting in the speaker.

"Nick!" he cried. "Nick!"

"——*in the doorway now!*" came the terror-shrill wail from the speaker. "Coming in! Oyster-face— great, blank, watery oyster-face—— Danny, Danny, put me back on the air, tell 'em all it's just a joke, tell 'em it isn't so, tell 'em not to believe, not to believe. Danny, do you hear, tell 'em not to believe!

"It's coming in! It wants me! It smells, and it's all wet and watery and its face—its *face!* Danny, tell 'em not to believe! It's 'cause they believe. It didn't exist. I thought it up. But they all believed me. You said they did! Five million people, all believing at the same time! Believing strong enough for you to feel! They've made it, Danny, they've brought it to life! It's doing just what I said it did, and it looks just like I——like I—— *Danny! Help me!* HELP ME!"

The loud-speaker screamed, vibrated shrilly at the overload and was silent. And in the sudden hush, an echo came from the night. No, not an echo, but the scream itself they had been hearing. Faint, and dreadful, it reached them, and Danny Lomax was quite unable to move for an instant.

Then he galvanized into action, and as he ran into the darkness, the others followed. With horrifying finality, Nick Deene's screams had ceased. Danny could see the Carriday house ahead, dark, silent, tomb-like. It was three hundred yards away, and the curve of the road hid it momentarily.

The three hundred yards took almost a minute to make. Then Danny, gasping, turned into the old carriage drive, Nick Deene's words still screaming in his mind.

"They've made it, Danny! They've brought it to life! Five million people, all believing at the same time——"

Could—— Could—— Danny's mind wouldn't ask itself the question, or answer it. But he had felt the currents of belief. In a million homes or more, five million people had sat, and listened, and believed. In the concentrated power of their believing, had they stirred some spark of force into life, had they jelled into the form of their belief a creature that——

Feet pounded behind him. Someone had a flashlight.

The beam of it played over the house, and for a moment darted into the darkness beyond and to one side.

And Danny Lomax caught a glimpse of movement.

A vague, gray-white glimmer of motion, a half-seen shape that moved with speed through the dense vegetation toward the four-acre swamp south of the house and for an instant shone faintly, as if with slime and wetness.

If there was any sound of movement, Danny Lomax did not hear it, because the scuffle of running feet and the hoarse breathing of running men behind drowned it out. But as he listened intently, he thought he heard a single scream, muffled and cut abruptly short. It was as though a man had tried to cry out with his mouth almost covered by something wet and soft and pulpy——

Danny Lomax pulled up and stood quite still, as the newspaper men and technicians came up with him and ran past. He scarcely heard them, was scarcely aware of them, for his whole body was cold. Something was squeezing his insides with a giant hand, and he knew that in just an instant he was going to be deathly sick.

And he knew already that the bedroom upstairs was empty. That the searchers would find only half a handcuff hanging from the footboard of the bed, its chain twisted in two, some marks in the dust, and a few drops of slimy water to tell where Nick Deene had gone.

Only those, and an odor hanging pungent and acrid in the halls——

Obstinate Uncle Otis

MY UNCLE OTIS was the most obstinate man in
Vermont (said Murchison Morks). If you know Ver-
monters, you know that means he was the most obstinate man in the world. It is nothing but the solemn
truth to say that Uncle Otis was so obstinate he was
more dangerous than the hydrogen bomb.

You find that hard to believe. Naturally. So I shall
tell you just why Uncle Otis was dangerous—dangerous
not only to all of mankind but to the solar system
as well. Yes, and quite possibly to the entire universe.

His name was Morks, like mine—Otis Morks. He
lived in Vermont and I had not seen him for some
time. Then one morning I received an urgent telegram
from my Aunt Edith, his sister. It said: OTIS STRUCK
BY LIGHTNING. SITUATION SERIOUS. COME
AT ONCE.

I left on the next train. Not only was I concerned for Uncle Otis, but there was an undertone of urgency in those ten commonplace words that compelled me to haste.

Late that afternoon I descended in Hillport, Vermont. The only taxi, an ancient sedan, was driven by a village character named Jud Perkins. Jud was also constable, and as I climbed into his decrepit vehicle I saw that he had a revolver strapped around his waist.

I also noticed, across the square, a knot of townspeople standing staring at something. Then I realized they were staring at an empty granite pedestal that had formerly held a large bronze statue to a local statesman named Ogilby—an individual Uncle Otis had always held in the utmost contempt.

Obstinately, Uncle Otis would never believe that anybody would erect a statue to Ogilby, and had always refused to admit that there actually was such a statue in the village square. But there had been, and now it was gone.

The old car lurched into motion. I leaned forward and asked Jud Perkins where the statue had gone. He turned to squint at me sideways.

"Stole," he informed me. "Yestiddy afternoon, about five. In plain view. Yessir, took between two winks of an eye. We was all in Simpkins's store—me 'n' Simpkins 'n' your Uncle Otis Morks 'n' your Aunt Edith 'n' some others. Somebody said as how the town ought to clean Ogilby's statue—become plumb pigeonfied last few years. Your Uncle Otis stuck out his chin.

"'What statue?' he wanted to know, his eyebrows

bristlin'. 'There ain't no such thing as a statue to a blubbery-mouthed nincompoop like Ogilby in this town!'

"I knowed it wasn't any use, he wouldn't believe in the statue if he walked into it an' broke his leg. I never met as obstinate a man as Otis Morks for not believing in a thing he don't like. But anyway, I turned around to point at it. And it was gone. Minute before it had been there. Now it wasn't. Stole between one look an' the next."

Jud Perkins spat out the window and turned to look at me in an authoritative manner.

"If you want to know who done it," he said, "these here Fifth Columnists, that's who." (I should add that this occurred during World War II.) "They took Ogilby 'cause he's bronze, see? Over there, they need copper an' bronze for making shells. So they're stealin' it an' shippin' it over by submarine. But I got my eyes skinned for 'em if they come around here again. I got me my pistol an' I'm on th' watch."

We bumped and banged out toward Uncle Otis's farm, and Jud Perkins continued bringing me up to date on local affairs. He told me how Uncle Otis had come to be struck by lightning—out of his own obstinacy, as I had suspected.

"Day before yestiddy," Jud told me, between expectorations of tobacco juice, "your Uncle Otis was out in the fields when it blowed up a thunderstorm. He got in under a big oak tree. Told him myself a thousand times trees draw lightning, but he's too obstinate to listen.

"Maybe he thought he could ignore that lightning,

like he ignores Willoughby's barn across the road, or
Marble Hill, that his cousin Seth lawed away from
him so that now he won't admit there is any such
hill. Or the new dam the state put in to make a
reservoir, and flooded some grazin' land he always
used, so that now your Uncle Otis acts as if you're
crazy when you talk about there bein' a dam there.

"Well, maybe he thought he could ignore that
lightning, but lightning's hard to ignore. It hit that
oak, splintered it an' knocked Otis twenty feet. Only
reason it didn't kill him, I guess, is because he's always
had such prime good health. Ain't been sick a day
in his life except that week twenty years ago when
he fell off a horse an' had his amnesia an' thought he
was a farm machinery salesman named Eustace Lingham, from Cleveland, Ohio.

"Your Aunt Edith seen it happen and run out and
drug him in. She put him to bed an' called Doc
Perkins. Doc said it was just shock, he'd come to
pretty soon, but keep him in bed two, three days.

"Sure enough, your Uncle Otis came to, 'bout supper,
but he wouldn't stay in bed. Said he felt fine, and
by dad, yestiddy in Simpkins's store I never seen him
lookin' more fit. Acted ten years younger. Walked like
he was on springs an' seemed to give out electricity
from every pore."

I asked if increasing age had softened Uncle Otis's
natural obstinacy any. Jud spat with extra copiousness.

"Made it worse," he said flatly. "Most obstinate man
in Vermont, your Uncle Otis. Dad blast it, when he
says a thing ain't, even though it's right there in front

of him, blamed if he don't say it so positive you almost believe him.

"Sat on his front stoop myself, only last week, with that old barn of Willoughby's spang in the way of the view, and your Uncle Otis lookin' at it as if it weren't there.

"'Fine view,' I said, 'iff'n only that barn warn't there,' an' your Uncle Otis looked at me like I was crazy.

"'Barn?' he said. 'What barn? No barn there an' never has been. Finest view in Vermont. See for twenty miles.'"

Jud Perkins chuckled and just missed running down a yellow dog and a boy on a bicycle.

"There's people got so much faith they can believe what ain't," he said. "But your Uncle Otis is the only man I ever met so obstinate he can disbelieve in things that is."

I was in a thoughtful mood when Jud Perkins dropped me at Uncle Otis's gate. Uncle Otis wasn't in sight, but I headed around to the rear of the house and Aunt Edith came hurrying out of the kitchen, her apron, skirts, hair and hands all fluttering.

"Oh, Murchison!" she cried. "I'm so glad you're here. I don't know what to do, I simply don't. The most dreadful thing has happened to Otis, and——"

Then I saw Uncle Otis himself, going down the walk to get the evening paper from a tin receptacle at the gate. His small, spare figure upright and a stubborn jaw outthrust, his bushy white eyebrows bristling, he looked unaltered to me. But Aunt Edith only wrung her hands when I said so.

"I know," she sighed. "If you didn't know the truth, you'd think it actually did him good to be hit by lightning. But here he comes, I can't tell you any more now. After supper! He mustn't be allowed to guess—— Oh, I do hope nothing dreadful happens before we can stop it."

And then, as Uncle Otis approached with his paper, she fled back into the kitchen.

Uncle Otis certainly did not seem changed, unless for the better. As Jud Perkins had remarked, he seemed younger. He shook my hand heartily and my arm tingled, as if from an electric shock. His eyes sparkled. His whole being seemed keyed up and buoyant with mysterious energy.

We strolled toward the front porch and stood facing the rotting old barn across the road that had spoiled the view. Grasping for a conversational topic as I studied Uncle Otis to discover what Aunt Edith meant, I suggested it was too bad the storm two days before hadn't blown the barn down and finished it.

"Barn?" Uncle Otis scowled at me. "What barn? No barn there, boy! Nothing but the view—finest view in Vermont. If you can see a barn there you'd better get to a doctor fast as you can hike."

As Jud had said, he spoke so convincingly that in spite of myself I had to turn for another look at the structure. I remained staring for quite some time, I expect, and probably I blinked.

Because Uncle Otis was telling the truth.

There wasn't any barn—now.

All through supper a suspicion of the incredible truth grew on me. And after supper, while Uncle Otis read his paper in the parlor, I followed Aunt Edith into the kitchen.

She only sighed when I told her about the barn, and looked at me with haunted eyes.

"Yes," she whispered, "it's Otis. I knew when the statue—went—yesterday when we were in Simpkins's store. I was looking right at it when Otis said what he did and it—it was just gone, right from under my eyes. That's when I sent you the telegram."

"You mean," I asked, "that since Uncle Otis was struck by lightning, his obstinacy has taken a new turn? He used to think things he didn't like didn't exist, and that was all. But now, when he thinks it, due to some peculiar heightening of his tremendously obstinate will power, the things *don't* exist? He just disbelieves them right out of existence?"

Aunt Edith nodded. "They just *go!*" she cried. "When he says a thing's not, now it's *not*."

I confess the idea made me uneasy. There were a number of unpleasant possibilities that occurred to me. The list of things—and people—Uncle Otis didn't believe in was long and varied.

"What do you suppose the limit is?" I asked. "A statue, a barn—where do you suppose it stops?"

"I don't know," she told me. "Maybe there isn't any limit to it. Otis is an *awfully* obstinate man and—well, suppose something reminds him about the dam?

Suppose he says there isn't any dam? It's a hundred feet high and all that water behind it——"

She did not have to finish. If Uncle Otis suddenly disbelieved the Hillport dam out of existence, the impounded water that would be set free would wipe away the village, and might kill the whole five hundred inhabitants.

"And then, of course, there are all those far-off countries with the funny names he's never believed were real," Aunt Edith whispered. "Like Zanzibar and Martinique."

"And Guatemala and Polynesia," I agreed, frowning. "If he were reminded of one of those by something, and took it into his head to declare it didn't exist, there's no telling what might happen. The sudden disappearance of any one of them—why, tidal waves and earthquakes would be the least we could expect."

"But what can we do to stop him?" Aunt Edith wanted to know, desperately. "We can't tell him that he mustn't——"

She was interrupted by a snort as Uncle Otis marched into the kitchen with the evening paper.

"Listen to this!" he commanded, and read us a short item, the gist of which was that Seth Youngman, the second cousin who had lawsuited his hill away from him, was planning to sell Marble Hill to a New York company that would quarry it. Then Uncle Otis threw the paper down on the kitchen table in disgust.

"What they talking about?" he barked, his eyebrows bristling. "Marble Hill? No hill around here by that name, and never has been. And Seth Youngman never owned a hill in his life. What kind of idiots get this paper out, I want to know?"

He glowered at us. And in the silence, a faint distant rumbling, as of displaced stones, could be heard. Aunt Edith and I turned as one. It was still light, and from the kitchen window we could see to the northwest, where Marble Hill stood up against the horizon like a battered derby hat—or where it *had* stood.

The ancient prophets may have had faith strong enough to move mountains. But Uncle Otis was possessed of something far more remarkable, it seemed— a lack of faith which could unmove them.

Uncle Otis himself, unaware of anything unusual, picked up the paper again, grumbling.

"Everybody's crazy these days," he declared. "Piece here about President Roosevelt. Not Teddy Roosevelt, but somebody called Franklin. Can't even get a man's name straight. Everybody ought to know there's no such president as Franklin Roo——"

"Uncle Otis!" I shouted. "Look, there's a mouse!"

Uncle Otis stopped and turned. There *was* a mouse, crouched under the stove, and it was the only thing I could think of to distract Uncle Otis's attention before he expressed his disbelief in Franklin D. Roosevelt. I was barely in time. I dabbed at my brow. Uncle Otis scowled.

"Where?" he demanded. "No mouse there I can see."

"Th——" I started to point. Then I checked myself. As soon as he had spoken, of course, the mouse was gone. I said instead that I must have been mistaken.

Uncle Otis snorted and strode back toward the parlor. Aunt Edith and I looked at each other.

"If he'd said——" she began. "——if he'd finished saying there isn't any President Roose——"

She never completed the sentence. Uncle Otis, going through the doorway, caught his foot in a hole worn through the linoleum and fell full length into the hall. As he went down, his head struck a table, and he was unconscious when we reached him.

I carried Uncle Otis into the parlor and laid him on the old horsehair sofa. Aunt Edith brought a cold compress and spirits of ammonia. Together we worked over Uncle Otis's limp form, and presently he opened his eyes, blinking at us without recognition.

"Who're you?" he demanded. "What happened to me?"

"Otis!" Aunt Edith cried. "I'm your sister. You fell and hit your head. You've been unconscious."

Uncle Otis glowered at us with deep suspicion. "Otis?" he repeated. "My name's not Otis. Who do you think I am, anyway?"

"But it *is* Otis!" Aunt Edith wailed. "You're Otis Morks, my brother, and you live in Hillport, Vermont. You've lived here all your life."

Uncle Otis's lower lip stuck out obstinately.

"My name's *not* Otis Morks," he declared, rising. "I'm Eustace Lingham, of Cleveland, Ohio. I sell farm machinery. I'm not your brother. I've never seen you before, either of you. I've got a headache and I'm tired of talking. I'm going out and get some fresh air. Maybe it'll make my head feel better."

Dumbly Aunt Edith stood to one side. Uncle Otis
marched out into the hall and through the front door.
Aunt Edith, peering out the window, reported that he
was standing on the front steps, looking up at the stars.

"It's happened again," she said despairingly. "His
amnesia's come back. Just like the time twenty years
ago when he fell off a horse and thought he was this
Eustace Lingham from Cleveland for a whole week.

"Oh, Murchison, now we've got to call the doctor.
But if the doctor finds out about the other, he'll want
to shut him up. Only, if anybody tries to shut Otis up,
he'll just disbelieve in them and the place they want
to shut him up in, too. Then they—they——"

"But if something isn't done," I pointed out, "there's
no telling what may happen. He's bound to read about
President Roosevelt again. You can't miss his name in
the papers these days, even in Vermont. Or else he'll
come across a mention of Madagascar or Guatemala."

"Or get into a fuss with the income tax people,"
Aunt Edith put in. "He keeps getting letters from
them about why he's never paid any income tax. The
last letter, they said they were going to send somebody
to call on him in person. But he says there isn't any
such thing as an income tax, so there can't be any
income-tax collectors. So if a man comes here saying
he's an income-tax collector, Uncle Otis will just not
believe in him. Then . . ."

Helplessly we looked at each other. Aunt Edith
grabbed my arm.

"Murchison!" she gasped. "Quick! Go out with him.
We mustn't leave him alone. Only last week he de-

cided that there aren't any such things as stars!"

I did not hesitate an instant. A moment later I was on the porch beside Uncle Otis, who was breathing in the cool evening air and staring upward at the spangled heavens, a look of deepest disbelief on his face.

"Stars!" he barked, stabbing a skinny forefinger toward the star-dotted sky. "A hundred million billion trillion dillion miles away, every last one of 'em! And every one of 'em a hundred times bigger 'n the sun! That's what the book said. You know what *I* say? I say bah! Nothing's that big, or that far off. You know what those things they look at through telescopes and call stars are? They're not stars at all. Fact is, there's no such thing as st———"

"Uncle Otis!" I cried loudly. "A mosquito!"

And I brought my hand down on the top of his head with solid force.

I had to distract him. I had to keep him from saying it. The universe is a big thing, of course, probably too big even for Uncle Otis to disbelieve out of existence. But I didn't dare take a chance. So I yelled and slapped him.

But I'd forgotten about the return of his ancient amnesia, and his belief that he was Eustace Lingham of Cleveland. When he had recovered from my blow he stared at me coldly.

"I'm not your Uncle Otis!" he snapped. "I'm nobody's Uncle Otis. I'm nobody's brother, either. I'm Eustace Lingham and I've got a headache. I'm going to have my cigar and I'm going to bed, and in the morning I'm going back to Cleveland."

He turned, stamped inside, and went up the stairs.

I trailed after him, unable to think of a helpful plan, and Aunt Edith followed us both up the stairs. She and I came to a stop at the top. Together we watched Uncle Otis stride into his room and close the door.

After that we heard the bedsprings squeak as he sat down. This was followed by the scratching of a match and in a moment we smelled cigar smoke. Uncle Otis always allowed himself one cigar, just before going to bed.

"Otis Morks!" we heard him mutter to himself, and one shoe dropped to the floor. "Nobody's got such a name. It's a trick of some kind. Don't believe there is any such person."

Then he was silent. The silence continued. We waited for him to drop the other shoe . . . and when a full minute had passed, we gave each other one horrified look, rushed to the door and threw it open.

Aunt Edith and I stared in. The window was closed and locked. A cigar in an ash tray on a table by the bed was sending a feather of smoke upwards. There was a hollow in the bed covers, slowly smoothing out, where someone might have been sitting a moment before. A single one of Uncle Otis's shoes lay on the floor beside the bed.

But Uncle Otis, of course, was gone. He had disbelieved himself out of existence. . . .

Mr. Dexter's Dragon

WALDO DEXTER found the book in the most prosaic of places—a second-hand shop. Not even a good second-hand shop. Just a dingy hole in the wall on Canal Street, east of Broadway, a region as commonplace as Manhattan has to offer.

It was a shop devoted chiefly to second-hand luggage and old clothes of the most depressing appearance. Mr. Dexter entered it in the first place only because a high wind had blown away his hat, whisking it in a series of eccentric leaps out of sight into a dark alley well supplied with puddles.

Waldo Dexter watched the hat vanish without emotion. He was accustomed to losing things. His hats blew away, he left his umbrellas on trains and in subways, and his glasses frequently dropped and broke. He was a smallish man, going bald, with an eager

glitter in his eye that denoted the passionate hobbyist
—which he was. His specialty was the collection of
books and manuscripts devoted to magic and witchcraft.

It was to stave off a cold in the head rather than
because he cared how he looked that Mr. Dexter turned
into the little second-hand store. There were some
caps in the window, and he intended to buy one. A
cap would keep his skull warm, be cheap, and wouldn't
blow off. Mr. Dexter was not an impractical man, for
all his eager absorption in his hobby.

It was very easy to buy a cap. The only difficulty
was to avoid buying half the contents of the store. If
Waldo Dexter had been a fraction more suggestible, or
the small, voluble proprietor a trifle more persuasive,
he might have indeed done so. Mr. Dexter, however,
was firm enough to avoid this sorry consequence of his
slight mishap. But he could not very well refuse the
proprietor's last impassioned plea, which was that he at
least look around to see if there positively wasn't
anything else he could use.

Mr. Dexter let his glance run swiftly over the shelves,
counters, and racks. Then, as if some magnetic quality
in the volume had drawn his eyes to it, he saw the
book on a low shelf, gathering dust.

The volume was not thick, but in height and breadth
it was about the shape of an old-fashioned ledger. It
was bound in leather, of an unusual purplish-black
color and a fine, unfamiliar texture. There was no title
or inscription. There was, however—and Waldo Dexter's small, gray mustache quivered with interest—an
inch-wide iron strap running completely about the

book, keeping it not only shut but locked. For a small, rusty iron padlock of antique design was hooked through a hasp where the ends of the iron strap overlapped.

With a murmur indicating an interest so slight as to be almost non-existent, and a gesture so casual that a word might have stopped it, Mr. Dexter reached for the book, brought it forth, and blew a fine film of dust from it.

"Hmm," he commented, and turning a lackluster eye upon the proprietor, shook the book slightly. "What is it?" he sighed.

It was, he gathered from the instant reply, a volume of the utmost rarity, the personal diary of a European nobleman of note, an intimate friend of Napoleon's. It had been found in a suitcase bought by the proprietor himself at a sale of unclaimed luggage from the various hotels. It had belonged to a European gentleman who had been so uncouth as to run out on his hotel bill—at least, he had vanished from his room and never been seen again—and so had come into the proprietor's possession with the utmost legality. He was holding it for a collector who had offered him a hundred dollars for it, but if Mr. Dexter cared to make a better offer——

Waldo Dexter sighed, and yawned politely, restraining the itch that quivered in every fiber of him to see what lay behind that suggestively locked iron strap.

"If it's worth so much," he inquired, raising one eyebrow, "why did the owner have to beat his hotel bill? Why didn't he just sell the book?"

Then, not waiting for an answer, he fumbled at the

small padlock. It proved to be not locked—the proprietor had picked it. Mr. Dexter swung back the cover, the iron hinge at the back moving with some difficulty, and as his eye fell upon the first page his heart pounded so with excitement that it was with the greatest effort he kept his hands steady.

The book was not a printed volume. It was handwritten in ink, with flowing letters so ornate as to be almost unreadable, upon ruled pages. The writing seemed to be a mixture of bad French and Italian, with some Latin thrown in for good measure.

It was not a diary at all, though the fact of its being handwritten might have misled an ignorant purchaser.

At the top of the page, in the bold, flowing script, was written in Italian: *Recipes and Conjurations*. And beneath that a few lines of verse which Mr. Dexter, because of their multilingual complexity, was not able to puzzle out. Beneath the verse was the single capital letter: *C*.

Waldo Dexter's pulse was hammering as he flipped rapidly through the pages of the volume. He dared not inspect it more closely, lest he reveal his interest. But his gratified eye made out, at the top of several of the pages, such tantalizing headings as *To Be Invisible*, and *To Make a Demon Bring Three Bags of Gold*.

There were others, equally promising, but his scholarship was not great enough to untangle the lingual mixture of their wording in such a brief space. He did, however, pause to study with gleaming eyes the picture which some hand had inset into the exact center of the book.

The picture had been painted by a skilled artist upon the finest of parchment. The parchment was a trifle yellowed, but the brilliant colors of the small, hungry-looking dragon upon it were undimmed.

It was a quite repulsive little creature, squatting upon a flagstoned floor, and staring out from the page with bright yellow eyes. At a slight distance behind the dragon the unknown artist had added a touch of artistic detail by putting in a cluttered heap of bones. Mr. Dexter did not try to make out more.

He closed the volume, yawned again, and shook his head.

"You lied to me," he accused the proprietor, looking him in the eye. "This isn't a diary at all. It's just a lot of nonsense. It's either an old copybook that some child did compositions in, or something similar. The picture's obviously a child's drawing. The whole thing isn't worth a dollar, except for the binding and clasp. If this was a real book, I might buy it, but just to put in my library as a curiosity. Even then I wouldn't give more than ten dollars for it."

He shrugged and started to put the book back. The proprietor brought forth a hasty torrent of words. Ultimately Mr. Dexter allowed himself to be persuaded. Having set his own price, he was eventually talked out of ten dollars. Presently, shaking so with suppressed eagerness he could hardly hold the paper-wrapped book in his hands, he emerged from the shop. After one quick gulp of fresh air, he dived into a taxi to be taken to Pennsylvania Station, and thence by train to Bayside, Long Island, where he lived comfortably in a small house close to the water, tended by an aged couple.

Arriving home, Waldo Dexter popped directly into his study, and there, with trembling fingers, unwrapped his treasure. He leafed through it, at first quickly, then giving close attention to some of the pages. He spent perhaps an hour in this preliminary survey, and after that, because he simply had to tell someone of his find, he took enough time out to dash off a quick letter to his nearest crony. This was one McKenzie Muir, whose residence was in the Bay Ridge section of Brooklyn.

It is (wrote Waldo Dexter) a hand-written volume of recipes and conjurations dating at least to the early 18th century. It is bound in, I am positive, human skin; a Senegambian's, I would wager. An iron band constitutes part of the binding, and this locks with an iron padlock. Within, upon the first page, is a bit of doggerel verse which I have finally translated as

> *Ope' not this book*
> *'Twixt dusk and dawn*
> *Lest you let loose*
> *The devil's spawn.*

Beneath that is the single letter, an ornate capital C. The warning I take to be intended to scare off unauthorized persons who might wish to make use of the volume. For—I have no proof, but hope to discover some—I am convinced that this was Cagliostro's own personal volume of magical charms and conjurations!

The whole thing is written in a hash of Latin, French, and Italian. This I take to have been an additional precaution against unauthorized use, since only a very well-educated person could possibly have read it. It will take considerable digging to make the necessary translations, but I have already partially deciphered two of the conjurations. One is simply called, "To Be Invisible." The other, "To Make a Demon Bring Three Bags of Gold."

If the ingredients were available, I would most certainly try the charms out! But one of the necessary articles for the first, for instance, is fat tried from the hand of a man hanged upon a gibbet. This imposes some difficulty in using the recipes! But I have no doubt I will find others which are simpler and then I shall positively experiment to discover their efficacy.

The most noteworthy item in the volume, though, is an inset parchment containing the brilliantly colored picture of a dragon. The monster has green scales, long blue claws, blue fangs in a crimson mouth, a scarlet tail, and scarlet filaments or antennae dangling from its head and spine like seaweed. Its eyes are bright yellow shot through with scarlet, and gleam from its head with an almost living brilliance.

The dragon seems to be squatting upon a tiled floor of stone, looking directly at you, jaws slightly agape, and a ravenous expression plain upon its features. Its scaled flanks are lean and sunken. Its bones show through everywhere. A leaner, hungrier, more sinister monster I have never seen pictured. I have, accordingly, decided to nickname it Cassius.

Behind the dragon, partially obscured, is a pile of bones—a pleasantly gruesome touch. For they are human bones. I have examined the picture through the glass, and there are visible thirteen human skulls, so skillfully done by the artist that under magnification every detail of them is accurate even to the discoloration showing some to be older than the others. Mingled with them are a mass of other bones and shreds of cloth; the whole is startling and almost upsetting in its vivid accuracy.

More than this I cannot tell you now. I have only had a few minutes in which to examine my find. Mrs. Studley is calling me for dinner, and I shall resume my examination after I have eaten.

You must come over and see it—today (as you get this) if possible. Please bring your collection of Cagliostro's letters—a handwriting comparison will tell us instantly whether this volume was indited by him or not. Don't try to buy it from me, though. Perhaps I'll leave it to you in my will, but you will never get it away from me sooner!

Cordially,

WALDO DEXTER

Mr. Dexter then sealed the letter, stamped and addressed it, and upon going downstairs to dinner gave it to Mrs. Studley to mail later. He ate rapidly, gulping down a really excellent meal, as Mrs. Studley testified later, and then dashed back to his study to resume his perusal of his odd volume.

When the Studleys, having cleaned up the dinner dishes, left for their own home, several blocks distant, he was so engrossed he did not even respond to their good nights—a fact which somehow greatly upset buxom Mrs. Studley the next day.

For when, the next morning, she sent Studley up to call Mr. Dexter to breakfast, Waldo Dexter was not to be found. He was not in his bedroom. He was not in his study. He was nowhere in the house. He was simply gone.

When the police arrived, they made slight headway in fathoming the mystery of Waldo Dexter's disappearance. He was just gone, with nothing to show for his going save a slight disturbance of his study. Some books had been knocked off his desk, as if swept off by a careless arm, and Mr. Dexter's glasses had fallen to the floor and broken.

Beyond this there was no trace of him. The disturbance was not enough to suggest a fight, and Waldo Dexter was not wealthy enough to warrant his having been kidnapped. The police finally decided that Mr. Dexter had either deliberately vanished for reasons of his own, or wandered off in a state of amnesia.

Neither of these suggestions could be improved upon by Mr. McKenzie Muir, who arrived during the latter part of the afternoon.

Mr. Muir, a lanky Scotsman, was not so much interested in ascertaining the whereabouts of Waldo Dexter as he was in getting hold of the volume Dexter had written him about. Quickly learning the facts, he did not think it necessary to show the police Waldo Dexter's note to him; nor, in fact, to discuss the handwritten volume which they found opened upon Mr. Dexter's desk, gave a casual scrutiny to, and put aside.

Muir favored the amnesia theory himself, and had small doubt that Dexter would reappear shortly. Before he did, Mr. Muir intended to see that the volume Waldo Dexter had stumbled upon was in his possession —and possession he interpreted as nine points of the law.

Accordingly, awaiting a favorable opportunity, he opened the purple leather-bound book and quickly slapped upon the inside cover one of his own bookmarks, a supply of which he carried in his wallet. Then, having given the mucilage time to dry, he took the book to the lieutenant in charge of the case. Convincingly he explained that his chief reason for calling that day had been to get back the volume, borrowed from him by Dexter. He showed the bookmark, and was presently allowed to depart with the ledger.

He left, filled with the exultation of the collector, and returned by bus and subway to his home—a trip of several hours, so that it was after dark when he arrived. In studying the volume on the way, all thought of Waldo Dexter passed from his mind.

Arrived at his own residence, however, Mr. Muir was forced for a time to abandon his examination of his newly acquired treasure. First he had to eat the dinner his butler had kept waiting for him. Then a neighbor dropped in and sat gossiping the rest of the evening.

When Mr. Muir picked up the book again, he found himself fascinated, as Waldo Dexter had been, by the repulsive little dragon.

After a moment he reached for a glass to study it more carefully. And doing so, he snorted, for he perceived that Dexter had been guilty of a distinct inaccuracy in describing the beast.

"'Lean and hungry!'" he sniffed aloud.

"'Bones showing through everywhere.' Gross overstatement. The beastie is not fat, to be sure, but his bones don't show through. And though one might say his expression was hungry, I'd not call it ravenous. There's even a bit of bulge to the belly, which is not an indication of starvation. And——" Muir peered more closely through the glass—— "there are fourteen skulls, not thirteen, in the heap behind the beastie. Ha! It's not like old Dexter to be so careless. No doubt he did wander off somewhere with amnesia. Must have been slipping in his mind to make so many mistakes!"

Noting that it was now close to midnight, McKenzie Muir hastily turned out his study light. He strode into his bedroom, found he still held the purplish volume in his hand, and set it down upon a bureau, putting the reading glass on top of the picture of the hungry little dragon.

Then, having extinguished the light, he did not give the thing another thought.

Even the crash of the reading glass falling to the floor some time later did not disturb him.

The disappearance of McKenzie Muir was really a

delightful sensation for the newspapers.

Since there was very little disarray—a broken reading glass on the floor, the bedclothes tossed in a heap into a corner—the disappearance was most mysterious, especially as the doors and all windows were locked. Resorting to the vague statement that they were working on clues, the police presently found it convenient to forget about the whole affair.

So the house was put in order, and the servants dismissed. It was Johnson, the butler, performing his last duties, who slipped the odd volume that his master had stolen from Waldo Dexter onto a shelf, and made everything neat.

As he handled the volume, it fell open in his hands at the picture of a small dragon. Johnson gazed at it for a moment with passing interest.

"Jolly fat little beast," he commented to Dora, the maid, who was pulling down the window shades. "Got a grin on him from ear to ear." Then, closing the book and putting it away, they left the study to gather dust.

The house remained tightly locked for some months, while some distant cousins sought to prove that McKenzie Muir was dead so that they might inherit it. Then one winter night a defective wire started the fire that before morning had reduced the entire structure to a heap of charred beams and powdery ashes fallen into the cellar hole.

And once again the newspapers received an unexpected godsend. The discovery of bones constituting the mortal remains of no less than fifteen human beings, together with some larger bones whose origin was obscure, pleasantly titillated several million newspaper readers for almost a week.

The scientists to whom the unidentifiable bones were taken were more than titillated, however. They were at first interested, and then vexed as they found themselves unable to come to any agreement as to the creature to whom those skeletal remains had once belonged. Eventually, however, they were able to salve their professional pride by announcing that the bones belonged to some hitherto unknown species of the sabre-tooth tiger.

So that, except for one small point, the authorities in the end were able to explain the whole affair rather neatly. The bones, they concluded, represented the victims of McKenzie Muir, a homicidal maniac who lured people to his residence, killed them, and buried them in the cellar. Undoubtedly he had so treated his unfortunate friend, Waldo Dexter. Then Muir, becoming frightened, had cleverly vanished.

Later he had returned to the locked house, to burn it and destroy the evidence of his crimes, and himself had perished in the flames—for easily recognizable among the grisly relics dug forth by the searchers had been McKenzie Muir's dentures.

Thus almost all the loose ends were cleverly tied up. The only point for which the authorities never were able to offer any plausible explanation was the question of what, exactly, a sabre-tooth tiger was doing in the house.

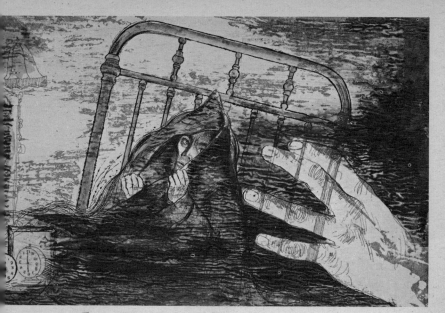

Hank Garvey's
Daytime Ghost

tHE BOY WENT CAUTIOUSLY down the path that wound along the slope of the hill, the moon dead above him. It filled the night with light, liquid and unreal, and peopled it with curious shadows. The silence was broken only by the boy's breathing and sudden small sounds as animals broke cover ahead of him and scurried away into the protecting darkness.

The boy gripped his stick tightly and pushed through a tangle of wild honeysuckle to come out at the head of an open slope down which the moon-cast shadows tumbled in dark, irregular array. At the bottom of the slope was a larger blotch of shadow discernible as a ramshackle cabin, walls leaning and roof sagging.

The boy gave a little sigh of relief. He hadn't been

afraid, exactly, but still the night was queer and the path strange. He'd come a matter of an hour through the dark just to find this place, and old Hank Garvey, to ask him a question. A question about a ghost.

It was a queerish question to come asking on a summer night, but it was a queerish ghost, what he'd heard of it, and he wanted to hear more. His Uncle Radex, big and square boned, had told him some, and his Aunt Susan more, quivering and shaking with the giggles.

But neither of them had made it very clear to him, maybe because they had laughed so much, so he'd come to ask Hank Garvey about it directly. It was Hank Garvey's ghost—that is to say, not the ghost of Hank Garvey, but the ghost that haunted Hank Garvey.

To learn about a ghost was an uneasy sort of errand for the nighttime, but the boy had an inquiring turn of mind. And though he was from the city, so that these Virginia foothills were new to him, he'd already become acquainted with the country. He knew there was nothing to be fearful of, save getting lost, which he didn't intend to do. And besides, Uncle Radex's and Aunt Susan's mirth had been a challenge to prove he was man enough to do it.

So here he was, and at the bottom of the slope was Hank Garvey's tumbledown house, dark and silent. But faintly in the distance the boy thought he could catch the sound of a voice uplifted in cracked song. Straining his eyes, he made out two shadows far up the opposite slope—shadows that moved, a large one followed by a smaller one. The large one he decided was a horse, so the smaller must be Hank Garvey, plowing as Aunt Susan had predicted, and singing to himself as he turned the furrows by moonlight.

The boy hurried down the slope, passing the cabin, and clambered up the hill beyond. Near the top, in the middle of a level field, half turned, he found a plow. But Hank Garvey and his horse had vanished.

The boy paused for a moment, breathing hard. Then once more he heard Hank Garvey's voice, off to one side where the incline gentled to the top of the hill. And after a moment he caught sight of the man himself silhouetted against the sky and the moonlight—him and his horse.

Hank Garvey was sitting his horse backward, riding the stolid animal bareback, and the beast was carrying him to the hilltop. The man's legs were drawn up under him on the horse's broad rump, and alternately he was singing a tuneless song and blowing tuneless notes upon a mouth organ.

For a moment the boy stared. Then he followed. When he got to the crest he saw them again close at hand. The heavy animal walked stolidly in a circle, loose harness straps flying, with Hank Garvey squatted like a Turk upon his back. After a moment the boy hailed him hesitantly. Instantly Hank Garvey leaped down, peering toward the boy as if poised for flight.

"Who is it?" he called, voice shrill, as the boy approached.

"I'm Johnny, Radex Anson's nephew from the city," the boy called back, his confidence returning as he came closer.

Hank Garvey waited for him, head half cocked, harmonica upraised. He was a little man, and his face was round, unlined, and very merry. Eyes as round as quarters in the childish face gave him an elfin quality, and all the boy's sense of strangeness was gone when Hank Garvey chuckled and answered him back.

"Hello, Johnny, Radex Anson's nephew," he called. "I'm Hank Garvey. Did your Uncle Radex Anson send you here on an errand?"

The boy shook his head.

"I came for myself," he answered. "To ask about your ghost. If you don't mind, that is," he added quickly.

Hank Garvey chuckled. Behind him the old plow horse had stopped and was munching the long, lush grass.

"Well, Johnny Nephew from the city," the little man said, merriment in his voice, "it's a pert night and I'm feeling spry and I don't mind a little company. If you've come all this walk in the night to hear about my ghost I don't mind telling you. But ain't your Uncle Radex told you about it before this?"

"Some," the boy admitted. "But he always laughed when he told it. I never did get it straight because of the laughing, Mr. Garvey. And I sort of wanted to know, I guess."

Hank Garvey clapped his harmonica to his mouth and emitted a series of discordant notes. Then he jumped in the air and clicked his heels twice, doing a grotesque pirouette as he came down.

"You sort of wanted to know about my ghost?" he asked, seeming vastly pleased. "Well, Johnny, it kind of seems to be dinner time and I've got a cold dinner hid under a rock here. Maybe you'll eat a bite with me while the moon looks over our shoulders?"

"Why—why, yes," the boy said. "I'd like to, Mr. Garvey."

"And I'll tell you about my ghost," the little man promised, turning over a flat rock and getting a tin box from beneath it. Then from the crevice of a split boulder he drew out a jug. He grabbed the cork in his teeth and twisted it free. Then he spat out the cork, caught it deftly, raised the jug, and drank long and deep. When he had finished he lowered the jug, slapped the cork back into place, and drew a ragged sleeve across his mouth.

"Aha," he said, smacking his lips with great satisfaction.

He chuckled and squatted beside the rock, opened the tin box and handed half a ragged sandwich to the boy. Johnny sat down upon a stone close by, feeling well at ease. The little man wolfed the other half of the sandwich, eating with loudness and gusto, and finishing the last crumb before the boy had barely begun.

"Now I'll tell you about my ghost," he said, leaning forward and peering at the boy. "But you tell me first, Johnny from the city, what your Uncle Radex has told you about me."

"He says that you've got a ghost that haunts you, and that you sleep all day and only come out at night to do all the things other men do in the daytime."

"That's right." Hank Garvey chuckled. He was squatting on his heels and he teetered back and forth. "That's absolutely right. I've got a ghost that haunts me, and I sleep all day and work at night. Your Uncle Radex told the truth. I get up at six in the evening and I milk my cow and cook my breakfast and do the chores. Then I plow, if the season's right and there's moon enough—but only if there's moon enough.

"And I plow and I sow. And other times, when I have some money in my pockets, I don't plow and I don't sow. Instead I climb the hill to look at the moon, and maybe I dance and sing in the moonlight. And maybe I go swimming in the duckpond, or just run—run up and down hills singing to myself because I like to. And then along about daybreak I go back home and milk my cow and cook my supper and go to bed. I stay there snug and sound till it's six o'clock again. And everybody says I'm crazy. Did you ever hear the like of anybody living such a way, Johnny Nephew?"

"I never did," the boy told him, interested. "Is that why you're crazy, Mr. Garvey?"

"Of course not!" the little man protested indignantly, and looked at the boy with solemn injury in his eyes. "Of course not. I do all that because I've got a ghost. Nobody could call me crazy for doing that because I've got a ghost. It's only because I've got a ghost that I'm crazy. You see, Johnny from the city?"

"Well, I don't know if I do or not," the boy answered, his high pale brow wrinkling. "You mean it's because of your ghost that you sleep all day and work all night?"

"That's right, Johnny, absolutely right," Hank Garvey said, bobbing his head. "It's the ghost of my granddaddy who came over from Ireland and was killed by his neighbors one day—but killed altogether by accident, for they never set out to do it."

As he talked he had finished off another pair of thick sandwiches and now he munched a great, raw turnip.

"You see, Johnny Nephew," he said as he ate, "my granddaddy was a contrary man—a *very* contrary man. He didn't get along with anybody, and he didn't care to do what anybody else did. When other men chewed he smoked, and when they smoked he chewed. When they went to church he went fishing, and when they went fishing he went to church. Naturally he got talked about.

"But he was a very contrary man, was my granddaddy, and he paid no attention to what the neighbors whispered about him. He went his own way and enjoyed himself his own way and those who didn't like it didn't say so out loud—not to him they didn't.

"But then it happened my pa was kicked by a mule and died of it. My mother died presently too, and it was along about that time my granddaddy decided that he'd rather work at night and sleep in the day, and he did.

"Now naturally that made him more talked about than ever, and folks began to whisper he was more than that—they said he was crazy. He wasn't, of

course—but that's what they said. And he took no
notice of it, but went right ahead plowing and milking
and hoeing and fishing by moonlight and making me
do the same.

"So pretty soon the talk became louder that I was
a very little boy and shouldn't be allowed in the hands
of a crazy granddaddy. People said I ought to be taken
away because he might do me a damage. So one day
the men got together and came over while he was
asleep in order to take me away and get me brought
up by somebody who wasn't crazy. And that was when
they killed him. They hadn't intended to do it, but he
sort of forced it on them by waking up while they
were taking me. So they killed him, before he'd done
more than break the jaws of two of them, and the
ribs of a third, and kick the eye out of another who
fell down and got under his feet. Then they took me
away and I was brought up by people who weren't
crazy but did all their chores by daylight. And that
was the last I ever heard of my granddaddy until ten
years ago when he came back from wherever he'd
been and began to haunt me. Have you followed all
that, Radex Anson's nephew?"

"I guess I have," the boy told him, never taking his
eyes off the round, merry face. "And then what happened, Mr. Garvey?"

"Well, Johnny, I had worked here and around as
a farmer for maybe fifteen years, and never cared
much for it. But I did it, and did everything everybody else did, though I could never figure much
reason for it except that I remembered granddaddy

and how the neighbors killed him all by accident. So I worked all day and slept all night and went to church Sundays and I voted. And then, just when I was getting most awful tired of doing everything like everybody else did, my granddaddy's ghost came back and began haunting me. And then I didn't have any choice."

"You mean your granddaddy's ghost *made* you work nights and sleep daytimes, Mr. Garvey?" the boy asked, trying to be sure he understood.

"Bless me, yes," Hank Garvey said, and chuckled cheerfully. "I had to do it. It was forced on me. Everybody understood that when I told them about it."

"That's what I wanted to know," the boy confessed. "Just how it was your granddaddy's ghost made you give up working in the day and take to working in the night."

Hank Garvey stared at him, round eyes wide.

"Why, by haunting me, of course," he said. "I thought I told you that. The only way I can get away from his haunting is by working nights and sleeping days. I thought I told you that."

"Yes," the boy persisted, "but I mean, *how* did he haunt you? Did he come to you at night, all pale and misty, and keep you awake and talk to you? Or did he walk across your room while you were sleeping and moan until you guessed what he wanted you to do? Or what?"

Hank Garvey teetered back and forth on his heels several times and then fell over on his back in the grass, where he lay laughing softly for the better part

of a minute. Then he sat up again and every trace
of laughter was gone from his face.

"Bless me, no, Johnny Nephew," he said. "I told
you my granddaddy was a very contrary man. Do
you suppose he would have an ordinary ghost? Not
my granddaddy! His ghost is just as contrary as he
ever was. Do you know what he does, that ghost?"

Hank Garvey leaned forward close to the boy, and
dropped his tone to a confidential whisper.

"That ghost haunts me *daytimes!*"

"Daytimes!" the boy cried in astonishment.

Solemnly the little man nodded.

"Instead of being pale and misty white, like an
ordinary ghost," he whispered, "this ghost of mine that
used to be my granddaddy is black, like an inky
shadow. And he haunts me by daylight. He used to
dog my footsteps all day long, lurking in corners,
creeping along beside me, sitting across from me at
the table, gliding along beside the plow, crouching
beside me when I ate lunch. It made me feel pretty
bad. How would *you* feel if you had a ghost haunting
you daytimes?" he cried at the boy suddenly.

"I don't know," the boy answered, eyes wide.

Hank Garvey leaped straight up in the air, clicked
his heels, and came down on the balls of his feet.
Nimbly he darted over to the split rock, drew forth
the jug, twisted out the cork, spat it into his hand,
raised the jug, and drank. Then he slapped the cork
back into place, hid the jug, and raced over to vault to
the back of the plow horse, startling the creature
from its browsing.

"Well, it isn't a nice feeling," Hank Garvey said then, warmly, peering down into the boy's face. "An ordinary white ghost at night is bad enough, but a black ghost haunting you all day long is altogether different, and worse—much worse. That's how I knew it was my granddaddy—by its contrariness. And that's why I have to sleep all day and work all night. Because when I sleep daytimes he can't haunt me—*and at night I can't see him!*"

He gathered his heels up under him and beamed down at the boy.

"Now you understand about my ghost," he said. "So come again some night when the moon's up and we'll talk more. But don't come daytimes. Daytimes I'm snug in bed, sleeping sound."

He laughed and kicked his heels. The horse broke into a trot. Hank Garvey snatched out his harmonica and began to play. Then the two were gone over the crest of the hill, leaving the boy alone knee-deep in fresh smelling grass, with the moonlight pouring over everything and only the sound of the little man's music drifting back to him.

About the Author

Robert Arthur had a lifelong interest in ghosts, haunts, demons, dragons, witchcraft, and magic. Once he lived in an old bat-infested house, where the bats would swoop around his head as he typed—just the right atmosphere for a writer of ghost and mystery stories.

By the time of his death in 1969, Mr. Arthur had written more than 1000 magazine stories, 500 radio scripts, and at least 75 television scripts. He was a story consultant and writer for the "Alfred Hitchcock Presents" mystery anthologies, and also wrote for Boris Karloff and others. His numerous books for children include anthologies of mystery and suspense stories, such as *Mystery and More Mystery* and *Spies and More Spies,* and ten titles in the popular "Alfred Hitchcock and The Three Investigators" mystery series. Mr. Arthur's work twice won him an Edgar Award (the mystery-writing equivalent of the "Oscar").

Mr. Arthur was born on Corregidor Island in the Philippines, where his father was a colonel in the U.S. Army. He began writing as a teenager and was first published when he was 16. After graduation from the University of Michigan with honors in literature, he worked as a magazine editor in New York City before turning to free-lance writing.